THE DEVIL
AND THE
SANIBEL SUNSET

DETECTIVE

Also by Ron Base

Fiction

Matinee Idol
Splendido
Magic Man
The Strange
The Sanibel Sunset Detective
The Sanibel Sunset Detective Returns
Another Sanibel Sunset Detective
The Two Sanibel Sunset Detectives
The Hound of the Sanibel Sunset Detective
The Confidence Man
The Four Wives of the Sanibel Sunset Detective
The Escarpment
The Sanibel Sunset Detective Goes to London
Heart of the Sanibel Sunset Detective
The Dame with the Sanibel Sunset Detective
The Mill Pond
I, The Sanibel Sunset Detective
Main Street, Milton
Bring Me the Head of the Sanibel Sunset Detective
The Hidden Quarry

Dark Edge Novellas

The White Island
The Secret Stones

Non-fiction

The Movies of the Eighties (with David Haslam)
If the Other Guy Isn't Jack Nicholson, I've Got the Part
Marquee Guide to Movies on Video
Cuba Portrait of an Island (with Donald Nausbaum)

www.ronbase.com
Contact Ron at
ronbase@ronbase.com

THE DEVIL
AND THE
SANIBEL SUNSET

DETECTIVE

RON BASE

West-End
Books

Library and Archives Canada Cataloguing in Publication

Title: The devil and the Sanibel Sunset detective / Ron Base.
Names: Base, Ron, author.
Description: Series statement: The Sanibel Sunset detective mysteries
; 12
Identifiers: Canadiana 20200305247 | ISBN 9781990058004 (soft-
cover)
Classification: LCC PS8553.A784 D48 2020 | DDC C813/.54—dc23

Publisher's Note: This is a work of fiction. Names, characters,
places, and incidents either are products of the author's imagination
or are used fictitiously. Any resemblance to actual persons,
events, or locales is entirely coincidental.

West-End Books
133 Mill St.
Milton, Ontario
L9T 1S1

Text design and electronic formatting: Ric Base
Cover design and coordination: Jennifer Smith
Cover photograph: Quinn Sedam
Sanibel-Captiva map: Ann Kornuta

FAUSTUS: *Where are you damn'd?*
MEPHISTOPHILIS: *In hell.*
FAUSTUS: *How comes it, then, that thou art out of hell?*
MEPHISTOPHILIS: *Why, this is hell, nor am I out of it.*

—Christopher Marlowe, *Doctor Faustus*

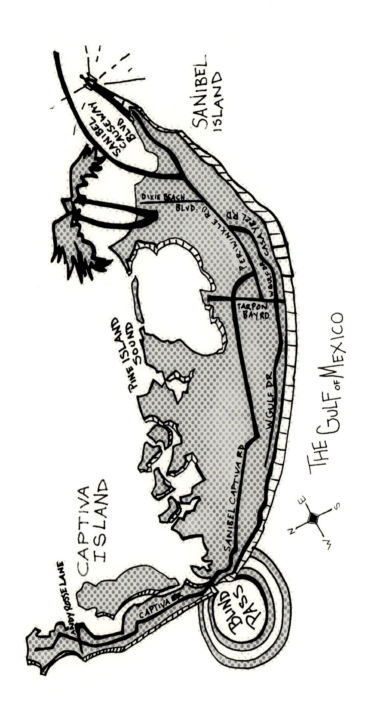

1

Later, he wondered if it wasn't a dream, something he conjured in order to explain what had happened. A dream made sense.

Otherwise, it was the black panther coming out of nowhere—or out of a nightmare.

Tree Callister was never sure which.

One moment the highway was clear. The next, Tree was staring into the pinpoint searchlights that were the eyes of the panther, reflecting the glare of his headlights. Tree hit the brakes and swerved hard right.

Suddenly, the highway was gone, replaced by the black of the night, everything moving in a blur until the Mercedes smashed against the fencing that was supposed to keep the panthers off the highway.

Tree expected the airbags to explode open as he was thrown forward hard into the strap of his seatbelt. But the airbags didn't deploy.

Bleary, everything aching, he had the presence of mind to undo the seatbelt, get the car door open, and roll out. The headlights lit up the mangroves and woods beyond the fence. Tree digested the fact that he had come out of the crash shaken up but otherwise unhurt. He turned to the roadway, certain he had hit the panther, and already feeling sick about it. The reports of motorists striking such an endangered species on Southwest Florida roadways saddened and angered him. How could people not see these beautiful creatures? They must be running them down on purpose. The panther deaths were an ongoing tragedy.

Now he had hit a panther. Now he had killed one of those creatures whose deaths he so lamented.

Except he couldn't see the panther. He went back to the car and got a flashlight out of the glove compartment. He crossed the road, looking for the body. But there was no sign of it. He began to think that he had swerved in time and had missed the animal. His relief was short-lived, however. Now he had to deal with the realization he was stranded in the middle of nowhere.

He went back to the Mercedes, got behind the wheel and tried to start it. The ignition made clicking noises, but otherwise the engine refused to turn over. He reached to the passenger seat where his cellphone was supposed to be.

Only it wasn't there.

Which is when he realized that after a meeting with a prospective client who had made him drive all the way out to Immokalee, he had left the phone on the counter at the gas station when he had tried to use it to pay—and that hadn't worked, either. He'd had to fish his wallet out of his pocket, find a credit card, and use that. In the confusion that surely was being brought on by reaching, ahem, a certain age, he had left the damned phone behind.

He tried to start the car again.

Nothing.

Worried now that he would run the battery down, Tree doused his headlights and got out. The pitch-black night loomed around him like a living, frightening thing. Would the panther return, bent on revenge for scaring the hell out of him? Were there alligators lurking nearby in search of a late-night snack?

What the hell was he going to do?

Not panic for one thing.

He noticed an opening in the fence not far from where his car had stopped. That's where the panther must have come through, he surmised. Beyond the opening, through the trees, Tree thought he saw the glimmer of something.

A light?

Could someone be camping out here? Someone with a cellphone?

It didn't seem possible. But still…

Tree went through the fence and promptly found himself in thick underbrush. That distant light appeared to glow brighter and so he went toward it, making his way carefully forward.

Soon the forest broke away and he found himself in a clearing lit by a wood fire that threw into silhouette the figures gathered around it. Tree moved closer and as he did, the figures began to understand there was an intruder. They parted to reveal a tall, slim man seated on what looked like an orange crate.

In the flickering firelight, Tree could see that the man on the crate was dressed in a black shirt and black jeans. He had an arresting face, long and narrow, with a thin growth of beard. His black hair was pushed back, falling to his shoulders. He smiled as Tree approached. Tree couldn't help but like that smile; it seemed welcoming, radiating reassurance that everything would be all right.

Was it? Tree wondered.

"Hola," the man said in Spanish. And then seeing who he was addressing, added in English, "Are you okay, my friend?"

"I ran my car off the road to avoid hitting a panther," Tree said. "Now I can't get it restarted."

The man traded glances with the others surrounding him. One of them looked at Tree and asked, "What about the panther? Did you kill him?"

"I think the panther is fine," Tree said.

The others nodded approval. The tall man stood and stepped closer to Tree, as though to get a better look in the uncertain light. "What's your name, amigo?"

"Tree Callister," Tree said. "I'm down the road on Captiva Island."

The tall man looked impressed. "Two things strike me immediately. First of all, your name. Tree. It is a very strange name. Not a lot of people named for a tree. Second, where you live. Rich people live on Captiva. You must be rich."

Tree shook his head. "My actual name is Tremain but somewhere along the way, everyone started to call me Tree. So here I am, Tree. As far as being rich is concerned, I'm the poorest person on Captiva."

"But the poorest person on that island is probably richer than all of us put together."

"I'm not so sure about that," Tree said. "But tell me who you are."

"I am called Lobo Salvador." The tall man held out his hand. Tree took it and received in return a beatific smile.

Lobo with a wave of his hand indicated the men around him. "These are friends. We travel together."

"Doing what?" Tree asked.

"You know," Lobo said, making another vague hand gesture, "moving around the country, going to where there is confusion. Trying to end the confusion."

"There is no end to confusion in Florida," Tree said.

"Everywhere," Lobo added.

"Do you mind if I ask what you're doing out here? Seems pretty quiet, not a whole lot of confusion."

Lobo's smile widened. "Maybe we are waiting for you."

Tree gave him an uncertain look, feeling increasingly anxious about what he had walked into. What were a dozen men doing in the middle of nowhere gathered around a fire that gave them a shadowy look right out of a bad horror movie?

Men who said their task was to end confusion. In an increasingly confused world, Tree would have said they weren't doing a very good job.

But he was not going to say that. He was not going to say anything.

"Do any of you have a cellphone I could use to get some help?" Tree asked.

"Sure, we will find you the help you need, my friend," Lobo said. "But right now, rest a moment, sit with me by the fire."

"I guess so," Tree said. The last thing he wanted to do was sit with this guy. But something told him to comply, and he allowed himself to be led over to where one of the men with Lobo was setting down a second orange crate.

As soon as Tree was seated, Lobo joined him. The others, Tree noticed, drifted away, seeming to have lost interest in their unexpected visitor. Lobo, meantime, presented Tree with another of the beatific smiles that had the curious effect of putting him at least somewhat at ease when nothing about any of this should have had that effect.

"I wish I could offer you something to drink," Lobo said. "But unfortunately, we have nothing."

"It's all right, I don't drink," Tree said.

Lobo laughed. "My father taught me that I should always be suspicious of a man who doesn't drink."

"If it's any consolation, I used to drink. I used to drink too much, in fact."

"And why did you stop drinking, if I may ask?"

"I was in the newspaper business in Chicago, and everyone I knew drank. Then I wasn't in the newspaper business and all of a sudden very few people were drinking. I decided it was time to join them. Not much more complicated than that."

"And yet you remain a troubled soul," Lobo said.

Tree looked at him in amazement. "How could you possibly know that?"

Lobo's smile was gentle. "You are here, are you not? And you are in trouble."

"I'm in trouble, not troubled. There's a difference. Besides, when you get to be my age, your soul, such as it is, isn't so much troubled as it is resigned."

"And you are resigned, are you, Tree?"

Tree groaned inwardly. If there was a time when he wanted a conversation like this, it certainly wasn't late at night in the middle of nowhere with twelve strangers and a car that wouldn't start.

"I'd like to think a certain calm has settled in," Tree ventured. "Although if my wife were here, she might disagree with me."

"And why would she do that?"

"She believes that in order to stay alive, I keep trying to get myself killed."

It was Lobo's turn to look startled. "That is truly extraordinary. A man who finds life by courting death. What does that mean, Tree? Are you suicidal?"

"The next thing to it, a private detective."

"Who tries to get himself killed."

"I don't try. In fact, I try to avoid it. But occasionally I fail."

Lobo nodded and, in the firelight, his long face had taken on what Tree later on would identify as an expression of enlightenment. "That explains why we have been brought together," he said. "Why we are here tonight."

"Well, we're here tonight because my car ran off the road when I swerved to avoid a panther."

"A man unafraid of death," Lobo said.

"You've got me all wrong," Tree protested. "Death scares the shit out of me."

"But you don't run away from death, you embrace it."

"Hardly," Tree said.

Lobo laughed again. "You are too much of a realist, my friend. You do not see the magic in the night."

"Tonight, I probably don't," Tree agreed.

Lobo rose to his feet. "Come along. Show me where you left your car."

"I'd like to call someone," Tree said. "It's getting late and my wife is going to be worried."

"We will get you on your way, not to worry," Lobo said. "But first let me see your car."

"It's not far away," Tree said. He stood and led Lobo back through the woods. None of the others followed. The forest and the darkness once again closed in as Lobo took the lead. Tree could see flashes of his wiry body moving ahead and followed those flashes until, thankfully, the fence appeared and not far away, the familiar opening.

Lobo was already standing by the Mercedes by the time Tree reached him. "You drive a very luxurious car for a poor man," he noted.

"My wife's," Tree said.

Lobo gave him a skeptical look before he said, "Give me your key fob."

"It's useless," Tree said. "I've already tried. The car won't start."

"Please," Lobo said, holding out his hand.

Tree pulled the key fob out of his pocket and handed it to Lobo. He got behind the wheel and pressed the ignition button on the dashboard. The car immediately started up.

"How the hell—" Tree said aloud.

Lobo got out of the car and shrugged. "They say I have a way with cars," he said.

"I can't believe it," Tree said.

Lobo was inspecting the front of the car. "You have some damage to the fender and it looks like the right headlight is out, but you should be all right to get your expensive car back to the very rich land of Captiva."

Tree pushed aside the insinuation that somehow he was a wealthy man. Instead of arguing the point—what was the use?—he said, "I don't know how to thank you."

Lobo came back to face him. "You must agree to do me a favor."

"If I can, sure," said Tree.

"Simple really, although for you, perhaps quite complicated."

"What is that?"

"Be careful," Lobo said quietly.

"Careful?"

"A visitor who will say he is the one thing, but he is not that thing."

"Then what is he?"

Lobo smiled. "In this world, you might call it evil."

"Okay," Tree said, trying to keep the cynicism out of his voice. "What would you call it?"

"Chamuco," Lobo said.

"Devil?"

"Whatever the language you choose, he comes and he comes for you, Tree."

"Why would he want anything to do with me?"

"He will try to use you. That is what chamuco does."

"I'll keep a lookout." Tree was trying to take this seriously, and failing. "How will I know when he arrives?"

"You will know, mi amigo, trust me, you will know." Lobo put his hand on Tree's shoulder. "*Que dios te ayude.*"

Before Tree could respond, Lobo had moved back through the fence, disappearing into the darkness of the forest.

"*Que dios te ayude?*" What was that in Spanish? Something like, God help you?

Yeah, that was it.

Tree tried not to think that sometime soon he was going to need God's help as he slid into the Mercedes and put it into reverse. The car backed away from the fence. He swung onto the highway, thinking about his strange encounter with Lobo Salvador.

Chamuco was coming for him? Well, that was nothing new, he mused. Chamuco had come for him in many forms over the years. And he was still alive.

But still…

2

When Tree finally got to the house on Andy Rosse Lane, it was after one in the morning. Freddie wore pajamas and a worried expression as she embraced him. "I never know whether to kill you or thank whatever gods there are that you're still alive."

"I'm sorry," he said. "I think I left my phone at a gas station."

"You did. They called my number, but that was hours ago. What happened to you?"

"I had the strangest experience," he said.

"Of course you did," Freddie said. "You always do."

"No, this was *really* strange. Unfortunately, it also involves the car."

Freddie groaned. "Not the car. Anything but the car."

"I'll tell you all about it, but first I need some water."

She filled a glass with water in the kitchen. By the time she came back Tree was slumped on the sofa, looking exhausted. "Tell me what happened?" she said.

He told her about the panther, running the car off the road, unable to get it started again, realizing he'd left his phone at the gas station, and then seeing the glow of the campfire through the trees off the road.

He related how he had made his way to a clearing where there was the campfire, not knowing what to expect, encountering the twelve men who appeared to be led by a tall, charismatic guy named Lobo Salvador.

"There was something magnetic about him," Tree confessed. "I can't quite put my finger on it, but you could easily understand why the others might be following him."

"Following him to do what?" Freddie asked.

"He said they moved around, finding confusion, trying to end the confusion."

"Now there's an impossible job for you," Freddie said. "Ending confusion."

"Well, whatever he's up to, he certainly came through for me," Tree said.

"How did he do that?"

"He got the car started."

"What do you mean? I thought you said it wouldn't start."

"That's the thing. I tried repeatedly and nothing happened. It was dead. But as soon as Lobo got behind the wheel and tried, it started right up."

"You couldn't get it started, but he could."

"That's right."

"What happened then?"

"That's when he warned me," Tree said.

"Warned you about what?"

"Okay, this is where it gets really, really strange. He said a devil was coming for me."

Freddie blinked a couple of times, digesting this news. "A guy named Lobo in the middle of nowhere starts the Mercedes you couldn't get started and then tells you the devil is coming for you."

"Chamuco, actually. He called it chamuco."

"Devil."

"Right."

He half expected her to laugh at him. But perhaps hearing the seriousness in his voice as he retold the story, she embraced him instead, holding him tight. "Tree, Tree," she said. "How do you get yourself into these things?"

"It's probably nothing," he said in his best comforting voice. "Just some weird guy in the woods, running his own weird cult, something like that. He probably says that to everyone he encounters. You want to get the attention of those you meet, just tell them the devil is after them."

"Yes, that would do it all right," Freddie said.

"After all, there's no such thing as the devil, right?"

"Aka Beelzebub, if I remember my world religion classes," Freddie said, "a figure in both Christianity and Islam, a fallen angel who seduces his victims into committing sin. Accompanied by acolytes known as demons."

"That's him, all right. Or her."

"Except…"

"Except what?"

"Well, in our contemporary thinking, the devil doesn't necessarily come up from hell to seduce us, does he? I mean, there's not necessarily one devil. There could be many devils. The devil's demons, as it were. He—or she, depending on your point of view—those demons can take on all sorts of human forms, right?"

"I suppose so," Tree said.

"When you think about it," Freddie went on, "you've met all sorts of devils in the last decade or so. It's amazing you survived them."

"Well, according to Lobo, I'm about to meet another one."

"There are, of course, those other demons."

"And what demons are those?"

"The ones in your head."

"Ah, yes, those," Tree said. "Particularly dangerous."

"Hopefully, the demons won't turn up tonight," Freddie said, rising to her feet and starting to yawn. "In the meantime, let's get some sleep. I'm dead tired."

———

Tree slept uneasily.

A prowling black panther loped toward him and stopped, its fierce eyes on fire. The panther moved off, past a campfire in the woods, mysterious men reflected in the firelight. Lobo Salvador gazed at him with a gentle smile.

And something else. A figure he couldn't quite make out, lingering at the edge of the woods, away from the firelight. Indistinct. Not moving.

That jerked him awake. He sat up in bed. Freddie was curled away from him on her side, sound asleep. Did he just hear something? Or was he dreaming?

He pushed the covers back and got out of bed. He crept out of the bedroom and through the living room, pausing at the front door.

Silence, except for the hum of air conditioning.

He opened the door and stepped outside into the warm, languid night, the air not moving. He looked down Andy Rosse Lane. He wasn't sure, but near the Mucky Duck he could just make out something. A figure? He wasn't sure for a moment. But then, yes, as he adjusted his eyes, there was someone.

The figure shifted around and then was gone.

The night and its silence pressed in on him.

3

Yeah, but how is the panther?" asked Rex Baxter.

"The panther is fine," Tree replied. "But your best friend in all the world nearly got himself killed."

"Panthers are an endangered species," Rex said. "Old white guys aren't."

"I might argue that," Tree said.

"I would argue there are too many of the breed," Rex said. "They need culling, particularly if they're out late at night on Florida's highways putting the animal kingdom at risk."

"You've got something against me driving late at night?"

"It's well known that old white guys can't see at night. They shouldn't be out on the roads. There oughta be a law."

It was lunchtime and Tree and Rex were seated at a table in a back corner at the Bimini Bait Shack. Tree didn't want to think about how long he had known Rex. To reveal that might make people think they were, well, past their due date would be a charitable way to put it.

They had met when Tree was a young reporter at the *Chicago Sun-Times*. Rex was already something of a grizzled veteran when Tree first encountered him. A former actor who had survived in Hollywood doing mostly small parts in B-pictures, Rex had finally deserted Hollywood for Chicago where he had become popular as the host of an afternoon movie show on a cable TV station. This was back in the days when such stations had to fill their schedules with old movies that no one wanted. As bad as the movies often were, Rex himself was vastly entertaining, keeping his meager audience enraptured with tales of his years in Hollywood. By the time he was finished with the show, there must have been someone in Chicago who didn't know he had slept with Joan Crawford, but Tree could never imagine who it might be.

Rex had been rescued from afternoon cable TV purgatory by WBBM-TV who hired him to be their weatherman on the six o'clock news. Rex, when pressed, would admit to knowing a whole lot more about old movies than he knew about the weather. But his Chicago audience didn't seem to care. By the time he retired, Rex had become a beloved local icon. Viewers had long since passed the point when they tuned in to hear about the weather. They tuned in to see Rex.

After he was down-sized—read, fired—at the *Sun-Times*, Tree and his wife, Freddie Stayner, relocated to Sanibel and Captiva, the pair of barrier islands hugging the west coast of Florida. That's where they reconnected with Rex. He had long since retired from delivering weather forecasts and had established himself as president of the local Chamber of Commerce—and was, naturally, fast becoming an island legend.

No sooner had Tree and Freddie moved into the house on Andy Rosse Lane than, against all common sense, Tree decided to open his own private detective agency. Rex sensed disaster but nonetheless helped out by providing Tree with an empty office inside the chamber's headquarters just off the causeway on Sanibel. Rex spent ten years meaning to collect the rent Tree was always too busy nearly getting himself killed to pay.

Now that Rex had retired from the chamber, the two shared an office inside the Cattle Dock Bait Company behind the Bimini Bait Shack. Tree continued to operate the Sanibel Sunset Detective Agency, despite entreaties from

Freddie and Rex to give it up. Rex, meanwhile, worked on writing his memoirs.

"Which I have now finished," he stated with some pride.

"Did you get in the part about sleeping with Joan Crawford?"

Rex blessed the question with an icy look before announcing, "I've got an agent."

"You've decided to resume your brilliant acting career?"

"No, no," Rex said irritably. "This is a *literary* agent. This guy's gonna sell my book."

"Who is it?" Tree asked.

"Jerry Delson."

"Jerry Delson," Tree said. "Isn't he in Chicago?"

"The legendary Jerry Delson," Rex corrected. "Jerry's not in Chicago any longer. Like every other white guy in America of a certain age, he's bought a condo down here."

"Here on Sanibel?"

"No, no." Rex sounded even more irritable. "He's up in Sarasota. He's driving down this afternoon to talk about the book."

"That's great," Tree said. "But isn't Jerry kind of long in the tooth at this stage?"

"He is, but then we're all, as you say, kind of long in the tooth. But Jerry's still got connections. Let's face it, all I need is someone to get me in the door at the big publishing houses. Jerry can do that."

"That's great," Tree said.

"You don't sound too enthusiastic," Rex said, frowning.

"I am enthusiastic," Tree countered. "I just wonder about Jerry, that's all."

"Jerry's fine. Jerry's great. Don't worry about Jerry. Worry about yourself."

"Why should I worry about myself?"

"A bunch of guys at night around a campfire in the middle of nowhere, one of them tells you you're going to meet the devil—"

"Chamuco."

"Whatever. Then he starts a car that you couldn't start and disappears. Not good. I'd be worried."

"I remind myself that having been in the newspaper business in Chicago for many years, I got to know many devils. In fact, I'm currently lunching with one them."

"I used to be the devil," Rex said. "Now, I'm too old. Are you sure you weren't dreaming?"

"I somehow got home, didn't I?"

"Maybe there was no panther and no guys at a fire warning you about the devil. Maybe you were hallucinating."

"Tell that to the body shop where they are currently working on the damage I inflicted on Freddie's Mercedes."

"I'm just saying." Rex was looking around the crowded restaurant as he said this. His face lit up. "There's Jerry now," he said.

Jerry Delson didn't so much as walk through the lunch crowd at the Bait Shack as he floated; a man in charge of his universe, a narrow face reflecting a lifetime of suspicion, thinning hair pulled back in a tight ponytail, dressed head-to-foot in the white of a good knight out to take on the world, the slight stoop as he floated suggesting the knight was somewhat beaten down by that world, but undaunted just the same. A leather man-bag was slung over his shoulder. You didn't miss Jerry Delson coming through the rye—or arriving at your Bait Shack table.

Rex was on his feet embracing Jerry, asking how the drive was, Jerry saying the traffic was shit but glad to be here. Rex introduced Jerry to Tree. They shook hands. "Tree Callister," Jerry announced in exactly the sort of raspy, Chicago-tough-guy voice Tree expected from him. "Private detective, right?"

"That's right," Tree said.

"Read about you in the Chicago newspapers," Jerry said seating himself and looking around, taking in his surroundings. "I couldn't tell from the reports whether you're a good detective—or a total idiot."

"I have always opted for the total idiot," Rex said.

Jerry was distracted. "What's that up there hanging from the ceiling?"

"It's an airboat," Rex said.

"An airboat," Jerry said, shaking his head.

"You know, they use them in the Everglades."

"An airboat hanging from the ceiling. Florida. You gotta love it."

"Can we get you something, Jerry?" Rex asked.

"Ice tea would be great."

"What about something to eat?"

"Love some smoked meat, but this doesn't strike me as a smoked meat kind of place. I miss Chicago's delis. I've yet to find a good place on the west coast. The east, yeah, you've got a few over there. But here, it's a deli wasteland. Ice tea's fine for now."

A server arrived to take Jerry's order. As soon as she was gone, Jerry reached into his man bag and pulled out a thick manuscript bound by a rubber band. "See this?" He held the manuscript as though presenting a piece of art.

"Rex's book," Tree suggested.

"No, no, you've got it all wrong," Jerry pronounced dramatically. "This is the entrance to a goldmine. That's what *this* is."

He placed the manuscript on the table as though handling a Dead Sea Scroll.

"I love this book," Jerry went on. "This book has best-seller written all over it. A goldmine."

"You think so? Really?" Rex, who had spent a lifetime keeping the excitement out of his voice, now couldn't keep the excitement out of his voice.

"The stuff about sleeping with Joan Crawford? Priceless," Jerry said. "And you with Hemingway and Sinatra on the Via Veneto in Rome. Great stuff."

"Sinatra was a jerk," Rex said.

"Sinatra," Jerry repeated. "Who knows what to make of Sinatra? But you nail him pretty good in the book, Rex." Jerry shook his head. "Sinatra."

The server came back with Jerry's ice tea. He ignored it. "Like I said, a goldmine. That's what we've got here. Sinatra. Joan Crawford. Great Hollywood stories. A goddamn mine full of gold."

"What are the next steps?" Tree asked.

"Next steps?" Jerry's suspicious face flooded with surprise, as though that hadn't occurred to him—or that someone would dare suggest it hadn't. "Next steps are simple: get this manuscript out to the big publishing houses, start a bidding war. Celebrity shit. Telling it all. Hot, hot, hot."

"A goldmine?" Tree said.

"You got it, friend," Jerry said.

Rex looked infinitely pleased.

Jerry suddenly sat back in his chair, his body rigid, his eyes at half-mast. For a time, he didn't say anything, to the point where Tree and Rex were trading glances. Then, finally, he said, "You know what I'm seeing?"

Tree and Rex traded more glances. Rex asked, "What are you seeing, Jerry?"

"I'll tell you what I'm seeing. I'm seeing... *movie potential.*"

"Movie potential," Rex repeated.

"Movie potential. Brad Pitt as the young Rex Baxter."

"Brad's a little old for the young Rex, isn't he?" Tree's question appeared to break the trance Jerry had fallen into. He sat up. "We find the young Brad Pitt."

If there was such a thing as pleased beyond the infinite, Rex was pleased beyond the infinite.

Tree left Rex with Jerry Delson and walked back to the Cattle Dock Bait Company, the thatch-roofed structure that was now the home of the Sanibel Sunset Detective Agency. Customers crowded the open interior in search of the right hooks and bait with which to attack the denizens of the deep in San Carlos Bay and the Gulf of Mexico.

He went through the shop to his office and stepped inside. A heavyset man wearing a blue blazer, his pale face framed by black hair that comes out of a bottle, looked up from where he was standing going through the papers on Tree's desk, smiled an all-too-familiar cherub's smile and said, "Brother!"

4

Tremain Callister, my younger brother," came the delighted announcement. The twinkle in the blue eyes went well with that cherub's smile.

"Scratch Callister, my half-brother." Tree did not sound nearly so delighted.

"Brothers-in-arms nonetheless," Scratch said. "And what a dear compliment, remembering my nickname from when we were kids. It's been a while, Tremain. Been a while."

"Twenty years," Tree said.

"Time flies away, old son," Scratch said, coming around the desk. "You don't have a receptionist?"

"You mean someone to keep visitors from going through my desk? No, I don't."

Scratch's grin widened but gave no indication he was at all embarrassed about being caught red-handed. But then Scratch's underhandedness never did embarrass him, Tree thought.

"The last time I saw you, we were both still in Chicago," Tree said.

"A bit younger than we are now," Scratch said. "But you're looking good, Tremain. Life in paradise seems to suit you."

"What about you, Scratch? Are you still in Chicago?"

"No, not for years, old son."

"Where are you now?"

Scratch waved a thin hand in the air. "Here. There. Everywhere. I'm something of a nomad these days, Tremain. A free spirit, you might say. Every day's a mystery, every town a new adventure."

The next question was the one Tree didn't want to ask, but he couldn't quickly think of anything else. "What brings you to Florida?"

The smile spread across Scratch's face—like oil on water, Tree thought.

"Florida is a vacation paradise, am I not right about that? Sun and sand and my long-lost brother. I thought it high time I paid a visit to the state and at the same time reconnect with you and your lovely wife." He paused. "Freddie remains your lovely wife, I trust."

"Very much so," Tree said.

"The woman who saved your life, you might say, pulled a drunk out of those Chicago watering holes you used to frequent, and made a better man out of you."

The years had not affected Scratch's ability to find just the right hurtful words. Tree made a Herculean effort to ignore the twisting in his stomach and the tension pouring through his body.

"I wouldn't put it quite that way," he said tightly.

"Oh, dear, Tremain, here I've gone and upset you and I've barely stepped foot in the door."

"You haven't upset me, Scratch." Tree could feel his heart beating faster. Shit. That was the last thing he wanted to feel.

"My intention was to deliver a compliment to you and to Freddie. Maintaining a marriage isn't easy. God knows you and I have had plenty of experience when it comes to failed relationships. It's good that one of us finally succeeded at that trickiest of businesses, matrimony."

"You're here on vacation, is that it?" Tree making a lame attempt to change the subject.

"A little relaxation, but business, too. Now as to business, why, Tremain, I don't know what I would have expected of you after you lost your job at the *Sun-Times*, you being such a creature of the newspaper world and all. But to wind up here on Sanibel, of all places, and a private investigator at that, well, who could have imagined it? Certainly not me."

Scratch paused, a sign that what was to come next would not be good. "Tell me," he added, "can you make a living at this sort of thing, old son?"

"A few dollars here and there over the past ten years or so," Tree said.

Scratch's bony hand was up and once again being thrown around. "I mean, what is this place, anyway?"

"It's a bait shop," Tree said.

"Not exactly executive quarters, if you don't mind me saying."

"This place does the job," Tree said. "I share it with Rex."

"Rex? Rex Baxter? Is that old ham still alive and kicking? Well, I'll be. Rex Baxter. Can't think of how many years it's been since I laid eyes on that old fart. Why he must be a hundred years old by now."

"Not quite," Tree said. "He'll be glad to hear you're in town."

"No, he won't," Scratch asserted. "That bastard never liked me, and I must say I always returned the favor. Weatherman. If the man said it was going to rain, you could be sure it would be the year's sunniest, driest day."

Tree just looked at him.

"There, I've gone and done it again. Making comments that come out much nastier than intended. I'm only sorry Rex doesn't like me better, that's all. Him being your friend, and you being my brother."

"Half-brother," Tree corrected.

"There are no half-brothers as far as I'm concerned," Scratch said. "There's only brothers. And you and me, we're brothers, Tremain."

"Whatever you want to call us, Scratch, it still comes down to the fact that we haven't seen each other for over two decades. I'm not quite sure why you've decided to show up now or what it is you think I'm supposed to do."

Scratch was all innocence. "Why bro', I'm not expecting much of anything from you. Well, that's not entirely true. A little hospitality, me being in Florida and all. Maybe an invite to dinner at the beautiful home that I'm sure wonderful Freddie has created for the two of you."

"Why don't you come to dinner?" Tree regretted the words almost as soon as they were out of his mouth.

"Wouldn't that be wonderful? Scratch said. "How about tonight? I happen to be free."

5

He more or less invited himself," Tree explained to Freddie when he got home.

"This is your brother, Samuel. The one everyone calls Scratch."

"Half-brother," Tree said.

"And he just turned up out of the blue this afternoon?"

"Rifling through my desk when I got back to the office," Tree said.

"That sounds like Scratch," Freddie said.

"He thinks the world of you."

"Your brother doesn't think the world of anyone," Freddie said. "Except himself."

"According to Scratch, I was a good-for-nothing newspaper drunk you picked up out of the gutter."

"Maybe, Scratch isn't so bad after all." Freddie was smiling when she said this.

"He's going to be here in an hour," Tree said.

That wiped the smile from Freddie's face. "I wish you'd put him off."

"Let's just do it and get it over with," Tree said.

"Remind me again, how it is you have a brother—"

"Half-brother."

"How you have a half-brother that I've only met a couple of times and you haven't seen or heard from in twenty years."

"Before my mother married my father, she was married to a guy in New York. The guy was older, had previously been married to a woman who fancied herself a healer."

"A healer? Did I know this?"

"I must have told you," Tree said.

"Why do I have doubts about that," Freddie said. "Anyway, go on."

"My father and his previous healer-wife had a son, Samuel, who everyone called Scratch."

"Okay."

"The situation was complicated by the fact that the mother had emotional problems."

"What kind of emotional problems?"

"They manifested themselves most dramatically around her belief that her son, Scratch, had special powers."

"What kind of special powers?"

"As a child, Scratch was struck by lightning," Tree said.

"You're kidding. That really happened?"

"It happened on Sanibel. The two of us were kids, playing on the beach. A storm blew into the island. It was pelting rain and there was lightning everywhere. I couldn't get Scratch to leave. He was dancing on the beach, screaming and yelling, waves crashing around him, thunder and lightning everywhere. Scared the shit out of me."

"And that's when it happened?"

"It knocked us both to the ground."

"But you both survived, obviously."

"I thought he was dead, but he wasn't. Scratch's mother, the healer, believed it was some sort of divine intervention. She began suggesting that her son was possessed. The story is that she even forced him to undergo an exorcism."

"You're kidding."

"Scratch would never say one way or the other whether that actually happened."

"Did it supposedly work? The exorcism, I mean."

"Who knows? I never heard anything. Scratch and his mother left Sanibel and eventually moved to California and lived in a trailer somewhere out around Joshua Tree. I never saw him again for years, not until I was in the newspaper business and he ended up back in Chicago."

Tree continued, "In any event, the few times I had anything to do with Scratch, I never saw anything particularly special about him, other than his ability to get under my skin."

"What's he doing back here now?"

"Scratch says he is on vacation, but there's more to it, I'm sure," Tree said. "With Scratch there is always more to it, and the more is never very good."

———

Scratch arrived promptly at seven, apologizing profusely. He couldn't for the life of him find a liquor store that carried the special bottle of Francis Coppola wine that he had wanted to bring to his brother and sister-in-law.

"Half-brother," Tree whispered to Freddie as he poured Scratch a glass of Freddie's chardonnay.

"Behave," Freddie whispered back.

They sat on the terrace, the sounds of excited tourists awed by the nightly sideshow that was the setting of the sun over Captiva rolling up the street, Freddie turning on the charm, Scratch reacting to it, saving Tree from having to single-handedly keep the conversation going. As far as he was concerned, he had nothing in common with Scratch Callister, never had. He found himself experiencing a combination of irritation, resentment and curiosity—wondering when the other shoe would drop and Scratch would reveal the real reason he was in Florida.

Meanwhile, he forced himself to focus, tuning into Freddie who, it turned out, was asking pretty much the same question.

Scratch was magnanimous in his answer: "It's like I told my brother this afternoon, Freddie, a fellow has got to take a little time off every now and then and so I thought I'd revisit the much-publicized pleasures of Florida, pleasures I'd not experienced since childhood on this island with Tremain. Plus, I thought it might be a good opportunity to reconnect with my long-lost family." He gave her one of his bright smiles. "And, sure enough, it is."

"And what is it you're taking time off from?" Freddie asked.

"Business," Scratch answered with yet another smile. "Always business."

"What kind of business?" Freddie, pressing.

"You might call me an entrepreneur, a risk capitalist, traveling the country, looking for opportunities, taking a chance on people, let's say."

"I'm not sure what any of that means," Freddie said.

"I meet a fellow, wallowing in confusion—or a gal, although it's usually fellows— not sure where to go or how to get there, but anxious to prove himself. A bit down on his luck. I take that person under my wing, offer support, end the confusion in his life and thereby get him back on his feet again."

"For a price?" asked Freddie.

That slippery smile, Tree thought, the one that appeared like a light signifying Scratch was struggling with a tough question but not wanting to show it. "Naturally, for a price—a percentage would be a better way to put it."

He looked at Tree. "For instance, I might want to invest in a Florida detective agency if all the indications were right, if the kind of help I could offer was needed."

Was that an example—or an offer? Aloud, Tree said, "Thankfully, the agency doesn't need any support."

"Lots of clients, have you?" Scratch asked, eyebrows raised.

"Enough to keep me going," Tree said uneasily.

"Well, if you ever need a helping hand, Tremain, you know where to find me."

"In fact, I don't." The words were out of Tree's mouth before he could stop them.

"Hopefully, that's all about to change," Scratch said.

Tree gave him a questioning look. "Why would it change, Scratch?"

"You know how it is, Tremain. Circumstances are unexpectedly altered. The fellow who doesn't need help, suddenly does."

Freddie slid smoothly to the rescue. "You know, Scratch, most people know my husband as Tree."

"Ah, but my brother will always be Tremain to me. Ever since we were boys."

"Scratch knows I hate being called Tremain," Tree said.

"And Tremain knows I hate being called Scratch."

Tension in the air.

"Would you like more wine?" Freddie asked, wisely changing the subject.

"I would never say no to a fine glass of wine," Scratch said, forcing the cheer back into his voice.

Freddie poured wine from the bottle in a wine cooler sleeve next to the table. Scratch said, "Now what about you, Fredryka? The last I heard you were taking the Chicago grocery world by storm."

"Not by storm exactly," Freddie said. "I was offered a job on Sanibel and Captiva operating a small chain of supermarkets. Tree had spent time here as a child. He had been downsized at the *Sun-Times*, I was looking for a change of pace, so Sanibel and Captiva seemed like a nice fit."

"And has it turned out the way you imagined?"

"More or less, I suppose. I ended up in an ownership position with the supermarkets. That didn't work out and now, as you can see, I'm a woman of leisure."

"Nursing your husband's wounds when he comes home from his various adventures, I imagine."

"There's a lot more to Freddie than that," Tree interjected.

"Of course, there is," Scratch said smoothly. "Never doubted it a moment." He looked at Tree. "After all, Tremain, Freddie is why the two of you are able to live like this, isn't that so?"

Tree gritted his teeth. Freddie managed a weak smile before she said, "I'd better see to dinner. Now play nicely you two."

"We're brothers," Scratch said again to Tree's increasing annoyance. "Whatever happens, at the end of it, there is always love. Right, Tremain?"

Tree tried not to choke on the bile rising in his throat.

6

It was nearly dark. The boisterous cheers from the sup-
porters of dramatic sunsets had subsided. Tree shifted
uneasily in his chair as Scratch gulped his wine. He placed
his glass on the table and exhaled loudly. "Ah, this is the
life, is it not, Tremain? Sunshine and comfort here in paradise with an excuse for work any time the inclination hits
you."

"Well, it's a little more than that," Tree said.

"Okay, fine, but you get my meaning." Scratch leaned
forward and moved his glass to one side as though to get
a better view of Tree. "Life's pretty damned good for you
is all I'm saying. I imagine Freddie came away from that
supermarket deal with a pile so whether or not you're out
there solving mysteries, you're still pretty well set up."

Tree looked at Scratch, not saying anything. For the
first time, Scratch's smile showed a hint of nervousness.

"Like I said before, Tremain, my mission in life as it
were, is to make things better for people. End the confusion that plagues the world. Do my small bit."

"You're a humanitarian, Scratch. What can I say?"

"Now I know you're putting me on a bit here, Tremain,
and I understand that. Me not known generally for my
humanitarianism."

"To put it mildly," Tree said.

"Still, it's my sense of altruism that brings me back here
to you. You see, I aim to make your life better."

"My life is good enough, thanks," Tree said coldly. "As
you've already been kind enough to point out," he added.

"But it could be better, could it not? All of us could stand a bit of improvement. You're no different, I don't suppose."

"What are you getting at, Scratch?"

"An incident from long ago that might keep you awake at night; a memory that still leaves you unsettled when you allow it to crowd your mind; a secret kept for so many years that you'd prefer to keep it in the dark where it rightly belongs."

"I don't know what you're talking about."

"Of course, you don't old son, and why should you? It happened so long ago, after all, safely tucked away at this point, except maybe featured in the occasional nightmare. But it's there, it doesn't go away. What you really are. What you should have been but rejected and tried to hide all these years."

"I haven't tried to hide anything," Tree said.

"I'm sure that's what you tell yourself, old son, and I can't say as I blame you. Who wants that burden, after all? But I just want you to know that I remember and hold it inside. After all I was involved too, although only peripherally, trying to help when it was far too late to help."

He paused as though waiting for a response from Tree. When there was none, he said, "There it is in a nutshell, Tremain, how I can make your life better, the way in which I am able to help you continue to enjoy the wonderful life you and the lovely Freddie have established for yourselves in this paradise of Sanibel and Captiva."

Tree gritted his teeth and asked, "What is it you want, Scratch?"

"You keep asking me that, old son."

"And I keep waiting for an answer."

Scratch blessed the response with one of his liquid smiles. "For now, a good meal with family members, a little hospitality shown to a visiting relative."

"And later?"

"Ah, well, later is later isn't it, Tremain? No need to rush things. I'm going to be around for a while. The sun. The sand. Friendly people. A body could get to like it in these parts."

They were interrupted by Freddie calling down from the deck. "I'm all set. Come on up and help yourselves."

"Be right there," Tree called back.

"I'm starving," Scratch announced, jumping to his feet. "I'm sure Freddie remains as fine a chef as she was back in those long-ago Chicago days. Yes, indeed, Tremain, you are a lucky man."

He started up the stairs and then turned to Tree, as though suddenly thinking of something. "Now's as good a time as any," he said, lowering his voice and leaning into Tree.

"For what?" Tree demanded.

"To let you know before things go too much further."

Let me know what?"

"I'm in love with your wife," Scratch said. "I'm in love with Freddie."

———

"You seem very tense," Freddie said a couple of hours later when dinner was finished and Scratch had consumed two bottles of Freddie's chardonnay before finally departing.

"I'm not tense," Tree declared.

They were lying in bed together, Freddie curled against him.

"Your brother certainly knows how to push your buttons," Freddie said.

"Half-brother," Tree corrected. "And he didn't push my buttons."

"I might disagree with you about that," Freddie said.

"Besides," Tree added, "don't all brothers know how to push each other's buttons?"

"I would say he's better at pushing your buttons than it is the other way around."

"He says he's in love with you. How's that for pushing a button?"

"Why didn't you say so earlier? Where's he staying? I'm packing my bags."

"Thankfully, I have no idea where he's staying."

"Damn." Freddie snuggled against him and began caressing his stomach. "I guess I've got no choice but to stick with you."

Her hand moved lower.

"Don't get any ideas about seducing me when you're thinking about running off with another man," Tree said.

"Never crossed my mind."

"That's not how it looks to me," Tree said.

"Things are looking pretty good to me," Freddie noted.

He drew her closer and for a time he forgot about half-brothers and dark pasts or anything other than the woman he loved and loved—and loved.

And, even better, loved him right back.

Afterward, he said to her, "There's something else I should tell you."

"Other than the fact that Scratch loves me?"

"Yes."

"Okay. What should you tell me? How much you love and adore me after we've just had great sex?"

"That goes without saying," Tree said.

"That never goes without saying."

"Scratch says he knows a secret."

"The world is full of secrets. Which one does he know?"

"About me."

"What's the secret?"

He looked at her. "Then it wouldn't be a secret."

"Tree, I'm your wife. We don't keep secrets, remember?"

"Something from my childhood."

"If it's a secret from your childhood, then it probably isn't very harmful. Not when you get to be our age."

"Scratch claims that he wants to make my life better."

"He ends the confusion in people's lives. He makes his brother's life better. This is all from being hit by lightning, I suppose."

"I'm not so sure he has any desire to make my life better."

"No kidding," Freddie said.

"I can't be totally certain, but I think he's trying to blackmail me."

Freddie raised herself up on her elbow, better to judge whether her husband was joking. He wasn't. "That seems a trifle melodramatic. After all, he is your brother."

"Half-brother," Tree said. "I don't know what to make of him. I've never known what to make of him. As a kid, he fascinated me and scared me at the same time. He seemed more at home in the dark than in the light."

"Before or after the lightning hit him?"

"Definitely after, particularly after his crazy healer-mother got hold of him."

"And performed the exorcism that didn't work."

"Allegedly."

"Blackmail. Boy, there's a word for you. Do people really blackmail each other? It sounds like the sort of thing that goes on in Agatha Christie novels," Freddie said.

"I hope I'm wrong," Tree said.

"If he is setting out to blackmail you, what do you suppose he wants?"

"I have no idea."

"Money? If I read my Agatha properly that's usually what a blackmailer wants, isn't it? Either that or the deed to the late duke's estate."

"I don't think he wants the deed to the estate," Tree said. "But I could be wrong."

Freddie delivered one of her trademark expressions of skepticism—an expression perfected over many years with her husband.

"Don't," she said, "hold your breath."

7

When Tree got to the office the next morning there was someone sitting at Rex Baxter's desk who was not Rex Baxter.

"Hi, honey, how you doing?" The woman at the desk was rail-thin with thick, russet hair framing a lined, been-around-the-block-a-few-times face.

A familiar face.

Tree said, "Blue. Blue Streak."

"You remember me," she said.

"From Los Angeles. The Bad Actors Detective Agency. How could I ever forget?"

"You've got that right, honey. However, since the time you were in L.A., I've had to dissolve that agency."

"I'm sorry to hear that," Tree said. "What are you doing here?"

"After we closed, I decided it was time for a change of scenery, so here I am in Florida. Incidentally, I'm no longer Blue Streak. Left my past behind. For too many years I was someone I never really was. Now I'm back to being my true self with my real name—Gladys Demchuk."

"Well, Gladys, it's good to see you again—you saved my life in Los Angeles. Are you here for a visit?"

Gladys gave him a quizzical look. "Didn't Rex tell you?"

"Tell me what?"

"I'm your new receptionist."

"Receptionist," Tree repeated, trying to process what he was hearing.

"Rex hired me," she added, as though that explained everything. "As you may recall, we knew each other when he was out there. The original bad actor, I might add. In more ways than one."

"Okay," Tree said. "But are you sure working for us is what you want to be doing?"

"Right now, while I get a few things straightened around, including what I want to do for the rest of my life, this is perfect."

"Except, I'm not certain we need a receptionist."

"Honey, believe me, from what I've seen so far, you need a receptionist. Do you mind if I ask what the two of you are doing housed at the back of a bait shop?"

"After Rex left the Chamber of Commerce, I needed an office, he needed a place to write." Tree shrugged. "And he got a great deal on the rent."

"I can imagine," Gladys said. "It looks as though I might have arrived in the nick of time."

As if on cue, the phone rang. Gladys picked it up. "Sanibel Sunset Detective Agency. How may I direct your call?" She paused and then said, "Tremain?" Her brow knit. "Oh, I see. All right. Who shall I say is calling? Hold a minute, please."

She covered the phone with her hand and said to Tree, "A Samuel Callister for you."

Tree wasn't sure how this constituted a need for a receptionist as he sat down and picked up his desk phone.

"Good morning," Scratch said. "That certainly sounds like an efficient woman you've got working for you."

"What do you want, Scratch?"

"Nothing more than an opportunity to thank you for your hospitality last night. A beautiful evening under the stars with fine food and a loving family reconnecting after all this time. It doesn't get much better than that."

"Incidentally, you never told me where you are staying," Tree said.

"I'm in the process of changing addresses," Scratch said after a long moment of silence. "I'll keep in touch and let you know where I land. Thanks again, old son. You and Freddie certainly know how to treat a fellow. And, please, remember one thing."

"What's that, Scratch?"

"Your secret is safe with me."

Before Tree could respond, Scratch hung up.

"Are you all right?" Blue Streak née Gladys Demchuk looked concerned.

"I'm fine," Tree said.

"That was your brother on the phone?"

"Half-brother," Tree said.

"Family," Gladys said. "Thanks to my nefarious past, none of my relatives speak to me. Saves a lot of pain and anguish."

"For now, what we've got to deal with, Blue—"

"Gladys."

"Sorry, Gladys. What we've got to figure out is what to do with you."

"Rex says that with all the publicity around this book he's written, he's going to need someone like me."

"That's what he says?"

Gladys nodded. "He won't tell me if I'm in it. Which makes me think I am."

"You and Rex."

"Bad actors, acting badly. He was quite a character in his day, believe me—even though he couldn't act his way out of a wet paper bag."

They were interrupted by two men appearing at the doorway. Both were dressed in dark suits, evidence that they weren't fishermen who had wandered into the wrong part of the Cattle Dock Bait Company. Big, muscular men, with identical brush cuts and thick jaws, Tree noted as they pushed into the office. One of the men had a mustache that somehow didn't quite fit his face. The other had a scowl that fit nicely. They didn't look like potential clients.

What they looked like was trouble.

"You Tree Callister?" the taller, clean-shaven member of the duo growled.

"How can I help you gentlemen?"

"We're looking for a certain individual," said the mustache man.

"What? You want me to help you find him?"

"In a manner of speaking, yeah. The individual's name is Samuel Callister," said clean-shaven man.

"We believe he's your brother," added mustache man.

"Half-brother," Tree said.

"We are looking for this individual," clean-shaven man said.

"Do you mind if I ask why you're looking for him."

"It's a personal matter," said mustache man.

"We're here so that you can tell us where he is," chimed in clean-shaven man.

"You think I know where he is?" Tree said.

"That's right," said clean-shaven man.

"I have no idea where he is," Tree said. Ordinarily when confronted by a pair of threatening thugs—and it happened all too often so he had plenty of experience—Tree had found he had to lie through his teeth in order to get out of whatever jam he found himself in. Not this time, though. This time the truth didn't help any more than a lie usually did.

"Here's the thing," said mustache man. "Either you tell us where he is or we kick the shit out of you."

"That won't help you much," Tree said evenly "Thugs with big muscles and pea brains are always threatening to kick the shit out of me, to the point where it gets boring. And even after you do that, I still won't know where he is."

The tension caused everyone to grow silent and not move. Mustache man said, "One more chance, jerkoff. Tell us where we can find your brother."

"Half-brother," Tree said. "But like I keep telling you, I don't know where he is."

Mustache man curled his fist and began moving around the desk to where Tree was sitting so that he couldn't see Gladys until she announced, "I don't think that's a very good idea."

Tree saw Gladys standing and coming around her desk with a gun in her hand.

"I think it's time you two got the hell out of here," she said to their two visitors.

While it was probably in the job description of the two men not to register alarm when confronted by a person with a gun, they nonetheless could not stop themselves from showing surprise.

Mustache man recovered first. "I don't think you want to shoot us," he said.

"Are you kidding?" Gladys said. "This is a stand-your-ground state. I come from California a state full of liberal pussies. But I'm free here. I can shoot you two, no problem. I'll be hailed a local hero."

Clean-shaven man turned to Tree. "Tell your brother that it's important he gets in touch with Mr. Custer Duckett as soon as possible."

"Who is Mr. Custer Duckett?" Tree asked.

"Samuel will know," clean-shaven man said. "Please, make sure you tell your brother that if he knows what's good for him, he will get in touch."

"He's my half-brother," Tree said.

8

Rex arrived at the office moments after the two visitors had departed. Gladys was still holding her gun. Rex looked at the gun and then turned his gaze on Tree. "I see you've met Gladys."

"We're just getting reacquainted," Gladys said.

"Funny," Rex said to Gladys, "usually people have to spend more time with Tree before they pull a gun on him."

"Two hombres came in and threatened to beat the shit out of Tree," Gladys said.

"Welcome to my world," Rex said.

"That's a bit of an exaggeration," Tree said. "I doubt they actually would have beat the shit out of me."

"Of course not," Rex said. "Just put you in hospital for a couple of weeks."

"They were looking for my half-brother," Tree said.

Rex, who had long since given up being surprised by anything concerning Tree, looked surprised. "Scratch? Is that son of a bitch in town?"

"He speaks highly of you, too, Rex."

"I can imagine," Rex said.

"He was in the office yesterday when I got back from our lunch," Tree said. "That was this week's first surprise."

"What was the second?" Rex inquired.

"This morning, discovering that Gladys is our receptionist." Tree nodded in Gladys's direction. She was busy putting her gun back in her purse.

"I knew I forgot to tell you something," Rex said.

"The question I have—and this is no reflection on you, Gladys—do we really need a receptionist?"

"Based on what just happened? I would say yes," Rex answered.

"Okay, good point," Tree said.

"Besides, I'm about to become a bestselling author. There's going to be lots of press, an international book tour. In addition to protecting your ass, we need Gladys here organizing my schedule, acting as a kind of gatekeeper when the crush of attention starts."

"I'm here to help," Gladys said. "I already like this job. The first twenty minutes and I'm pulling a gun out of my purse."

"We're hiring Gladys fulltime, are we?" Tree asked.

"Is there any other way?" Rex said.

"I'm a little nervous about Gladys and that gun in her purse," Tree said.

"What are you nervous about?" Gladys asked.

"Having a gun in the office."

"I'd say it came in pretty handy a few minutes ago," Gladys said.

Tree could hardly argue with that.

"Why don't we say that Gladys only pulls out her gun when someone is about to kill you?" Rex said. "I think that's a fair tradeoff."

"Sounds good to me," Gladys said.

"All this comes from Jerry Delson, I suppose," Tree said.

"The book is a goldmine," Rex said.

"So Jerry says."

"Jerry's been around the publishing block many, many times. He knows what he's talking about."

"I'm sure he does."

Rex eyed Tree narrowly. "I don't think you like Jerry."

"I like Jerry just fine. I simply wonder if he should get too carried away before there's even a publisher."

"Why don't we let Jerry take care of the publishing end of things?" Rex said. "Meanwhile, from what I can see, you've got your hands full dealing with your no-good brother."

"Half-brother," corrected Gladys. She was learning fast, Tree thought.

"Whatever. What's it been? Twenty years since you've seen the guy?"

"He came to dinner last night," Tree said.

Rex rolled his eyes. "What was that like?"

"Unless I miss my guess, he tried to blackmail me," Tree said.

"It's reassuring to know the years haven't changed Scratch," Rex said.

"He says they have."

"Yeah? How's that?"

"He's now trying to end confusion and make life better for everyone."

"Yeah, and I was the number-one box-office star in Hollywood," Rex said. "What's he got on you, anyway?"

"It happened before you and I met," Tree said.

"Before the earth cooled," Rex said.

"It's no big deal," Tree said.

"Is that your way of saying you don't want to tell me what it is?"

"If you gentlemen need a private moment together, I can go out for coffee," Gladys said.

"No, it's all right," Tree said.

"Do you know where Scratch is?" asked Rex.

"He was vague about that," Tree said.

"Well, you'd better find him," Rex said. "Judging by what happened this morning, Scratch is, as usual, in trouble—even more trouble than his brother."

"Half-brother," Tree said.

9

Tree told himself he was doing nothing more than keeping Gladys busy by getting her to phone around area hotels and resorts in hopes of finding where Scratch was staying. He told himself that he shouldn't get involved, that whatever trouble his brother—his half-brother—was in, it was his problem not Tree's.

"Besides," said Rex, seeming to read his friend's mind, "Scratch is like a bad penny. He's bound to turn up."

"Is that what a bad penny does?"

"I think Tree is worried that those two hoods will get to him first," Gladys interjected helpfully.

Jerry Delson came into the office. His eyes lit up when Rex introduced him to Gladys. "Why do you look familiar?"

"You may know me better as Blue Streak," Gladys said.

"No kidding." Jerry's eyes lit up even more. "*You're* Blue Streak?"

"I used to be Blue Streak a long time ago. Now I'm back to being who I was originally, Gladys Demchuk."

"There's a book here," Jerry said.

That made Rex frown. "Let's get my book published first," he said.

Jerry finally tore his eyes away from Gladys and focused on Rex. "Hey, job one, no doubt about it. I've got submissions ready to go out to the big five houses. I'm giving them seven business days to respond. We should be into a bidding war by the end of next week."

"That's quick," Tree said.

"Hey, we got a hot book here," Jerry said. "When you've got a hot book, you strike while the book is hot. And, pal, this book is *hot*."

"A goldmine," added Tree.

"You got it, friend."

He returned his gaze to Gladys. "Blue Streak. Wow. You had quite a run in the industry, didn't you?"

"Like I said, it was a long time ago." Gladys looked uncharacteristically nervous.

"Sure, sure, but in the heyday of adult films you were the biggest star, right?"

"People knew who I was, that's for sure."

"We should talk. I'm going back to Sarasota this afternoon to be in position to oversee the auction." He fished a card out of his pocket and handed it to her. "Let's keep in touch, Blue."

"It's Gladys now."

"Yeah, of course. Gladys."

She frowned at the card. "I'm not very interested in writing a book. I moved on a long time ago."

"Like I said, we'll talk, no pressure." Jerry went over and embraced Rex. "I love you, big guy. We're going to get rich together."

"If you say so, Jerry," Rex said.

"I don't say so. I *know* so."

Rex beamed as Jerry made his exit.

———

It took Gladys little more than an hour to track down Scratch. A Samuel Callister was registered at the Blue Parrot Motel off East Gulf Drive on Sanibel Island.

"Would you like me to drive over there, see what he's up to?" Gladys asked.

Tree thought of Gladys on Sanibel confronting Scratch with a gun in her purse and shook his head. "No, I'd better take care of this myself," he said.

"I'm here if you need backup," Gladys said.

Tree was outside before he remembered Freddie had the Mercedes today. To his wife's increasing irritation he had yet to buy another car following the untimely death of his beloved old Volkswagen Beetle.

He went back inside and watched Rex roll his eyes. "What kind of private detective doesn't have a car, and in Florida of all places?"

"That Beetle was like a family member," Tree said. "It was a death in the family, the end of that car. I'm still in mourning. Besides, I have a car."

"Your wife's car," Rex countered.

"Here, take mine." Gladys threw him a set of keys. "The pickup truck outside."

"Thanks," Tree said.

"It's a bit of a mess. I was kind of living in it driving from California to Florida, but it goes forward and backward—and the brakes work. More or less."

The truck Gladys drove was a dented 1972 Chevrolet, sea foam green, according to her; a sickly green in Tree's estimation. It was customized with wavelike blue flames emblazoned along its sides. When he turned the ignition, an engine that sounded like something coming out of the gate at the Daytona 500 howled to life, scaring the wits out of him.

Whether he had wits to lose at this point was debatable. If he had any brains, he wouldn't be driving over the causeway to—well, to do what about his half-brother? Warn him, Tree supposed. And maybe—since he had nearly gotten beaten up because of Scratch—find out why goons in expensive suits were looking for him.

At noontime there was a lineup at the tollbooth getting onto the causeway and then stop-and-go traffic all the way across. Seagulls swooped and hovered in the warm air above the causeway as though mocking the humans in their metal machines jammed together unmoving on the bridge. Ospreys mounted on posts gazed uncomprehendingly at the traffic. Tree was with the ospreys and the seagulls. Only humans would be crazy enough to be stranded out here. Mad dogs and visiting tourists out in the midday sun—and Tree Callister stupidly in search of a half-brother he should have nothing to do with.

The traffic broke up a bit once he reached the island, got off Causeway Boulevard and crossed Periwinkle Way onto Lindgren where there was even less traffic to East Gulf Drive and the Blue Parrot Motel.

A narrow drive led to the pink façade of the Blue Parrot, in the glare of early afternoon sunlight suggesting a 1950s Florida that had all but disappeared. But here it was on Sanibel where in places they were still shaking off the 1950s.

Tree parked in the lot adjacent to the motel, not far from a familiar-looking Mercedes.

No, Tree thought, it couldn't be. But it was. He would know it anywhere, particularly since the work done on the front of the car as a result of his black panther misadventure was all-too evident.

His wife Freddie's Mercedes.

10

Tree was about to get out of the truck when Freddie herself emerged from the motel. She wore white shorts and a matching linen blouse, emotionless behind dark glasses. She looked spectacular, Tree thought as she made her way to the Mercedes and got in, paying no attention to a sickly green Chevrolet pickup with blue flames running along its sides.

He watched as Freddie pulled out of the lot and sped away on East Gulf Drive. He was in the midst of sitting there, numbly digesting the spectacle of his wife exiting the motel where his brother—his half-brother—was staying.

The half-brother who had announced the night before that he was in love with his wife.

He was processing all this through a blur of confusion and anger when Scratch Callister emerged into the sunlight, a white knight in gleaming linen: linen slacks, a billowing linen shirt topped by a white Borsalino hat hiding that artificially colored hair. No cargo shorts and baseball cap for this dude, Tree thought. Could Freddie be attracted to a guy in a Borsalino hat on Sanibel? A guy who dyed his hair? Tree didn't think so, but then, in the end, what did he know about anything? The older he got the more he was convinced he knew nothing.

Maybe not even about Freddie.

By now, Scratch was opening the door of a black Porsche and sliding behind the wheel. Tree thought about jumping out and intercepting him before he drove away.

But by the time he debated the issue with himself, Scratch was turning the Porsche onto the roadway.

Scratch in his Porsche crossed the causeway then proceeded along McGregor as it became a palm-lined thoroughfare past the Edison and Ford Winter Estates to the reconditioned art deco facades of downtown Fort Myers. He made a slight right jog onto Victoria Avenue and then a left onto Cleveland, crossing into North Fort Myers, seemingly in no hurry to get anywhere. A right onto Bayshore Road and then a long haul to a massive concrete monolith rising out of nowhere: The Lee Civic Center.

Where a gun show was in progress.

Scratch turned the Porsche into the parking lot. By the time Tree found a space, his half-brother was out and headed toward the main entrance, an apparition in white joining a more anonymous throng favoring the baseball cap over the Borsalino. A big yellow sign warned that all weapons must be unloaded before entering the building.

There was a lineup for hot dogs at a food truck the crowd had to pass before reaching a long portico over a walkway where a vendor sold kettle corn. At the end of the walkway an attendant and a police officer were positioned behind a table.

The attendant smiled at Tree as he paid the eleven-dollar admission fee and then asked, "Are you armed?"

Tree said he wasn't, but supposing he was?

"That's all right," said the police officer. "As long as your gun isn't loaded. Why, we checked in six hundred guns yesterday."

"Lots of folks bring their firearms to sell or to trade," the attendant said. "Most times more guns go in than come out."

Having assured the two men he posed no threat to the Lee County gun culture, Tree entered a vast hall filled with long tables displaying more firearms than he had ever seen in one place in his life. A combination war room and arsenal, the bizarre uniqueness of a Florida gun show was on full display as normal, everyday business, attended in the same fashion anyone would visit a flea market, except this market was full of products used for killing people.

"You a Florida property-owner, sir? Or a taxpayer?" A young vendor behind a trestle table packed with handguns had noticed Tree standing nearby.

"As a matter of fact, I am," Tree said.

"Then, not to worry sir, as long as you can show identification and are willing to wait three days, you are more than welcome to buy any one of these here guns."

Tree thanked him and moved into the hall, looking for Scratch. A sign announced that he could buy, sell or trade his gun for instant cash. Good to know, Tree thought. Remanufactured ammo, whatever that was, assault rifles—expensive to own an assault rifle, Tree thought—gleaming lethal-looking hunting knives to be used to do what? Skin your victim after you've shot him?

You could buy a T-shirt that pointed out "The problem is not guns. It's hearts without God. Homes without discipline. Courts without justice." A woman's T-shirt with spaghetti straps: "Concealed weapons. But my man prefers open carry at home." Tree thought about buying the shirt for Freddie and then immediately dismissed the idea.

Tree stopped to inspect a display of brass knuckles that he thought might come in handy dealing with Scratch. Even better, a woman showed him a stun device that she said could deliver two hundred and thirty million volts of electricity. "It will knock down your assailant but won't kill him."

Tree resisted the urge to buy the device right there on the spot.

He finally spotted Scratch at the back of the hall, his white linen like a flag of surrender in a sea of shorts and baseball caps. He was talking to two men in dark suits. The same kind of suits as had appeared at Tree's office but different men this time, older, in their sixties. One of the men had dark hair and a thick mustache. The other was completely bald. Their expressions were similarly intense as they listened, heads bowed, to the equally intense Scratch. Nobody looked very happy.

As Tree watched, the bald man stepped behind a counter in front of a banner that said BlackHeart. On the banner, a lightning bolt cracked a black heart in two. Below the heart were three words: Confusion. Confrontation. Disruption.

The bald man rummaged in a rubber bin set on a folding chair and pulled out a gym bag that he then handed to Scratch. The two men looked unhappier than ever as Scratch smiled and offered his hand. Neither of the men took it.

Scratch lowered his hand, said something to the two men and then walked away, lugging the gym bag. The two men grimly followed him with their eyes until he ducked out through an open curtain and disappeared.

Tree crossed the floor and found himself in a dark walkway. There was no sign of Scratch. There were however two burly guys in baseball caps coming up behind him. One of them said, "Hey," before he pushed Tree against the wall and jammed a gun into his side.

"I don't know whether you're aware of it," Tree said. "But you're not supposed to have a loaded gun at the gun show."

"No shit," said the guy with the gun. "I didn't know that. I'll try to remember it the next time."

"But for now," said the second burly guy, "why don't you come with us?"

"Why should I do that?" Tree asked.

"Because if you come quietly we won't have to shoot you," said the second burly guy.

"Can you shoot someone at a gun show?"

"Sure you can," the second burly guy said. "It's Florida. You're allowed to shoot anyone anywhere."

The guy with the gun jerked Tree away from the wall and said, "Let's go for a walk."

11

A white van was parked at the rear of the civic center. As Tree was led toward it, the side-panel door opened, a gaping black hole that he had been tossed into far too many times over the years. Enough was enough.

"I'm not getting in there," Tree announced.

"Yeah, you are." The guy with the gun jammed the barrel into Tree's ribs.

"I've been pushed around by too many big, mean guys who never finished high school," Tree said. "I'm not going to take it anymore."

"I'm sorry to hear that," said the guy with the gun. "If it's any consolation, I graduated from high school."

"So here you are in a parking lot earning a living by threatening to shoot people," Tree said.

"Sometimes it goes beyond a threat," said the second burly guy.

"That's when I get paid more," the guy with the gun said.

"If you shoot me out here beside this van I won't get into, it's nothing more than a good payday for you, is that it?" Tree asked.

"Actually, I lied to you in there," the guy with the gun admitted. "I probably won't shoot you this afternoon. Instead, I'll pistol-whip the shit out of you first and while you're trying to pick your teeth off the pavement, I'll throw you into the van."

"Where are you taking me?"

"Where do you think we're taking you," said the second burly guy. "Where do guys like us usually take you?"

"They take me for a ride."

"There you go," said the second burly guy. "That's exactly what we're going to do."

Tree climbed into the van, the burly guy with the gun was right behind him. A thin-faced kid with pimples gleaming in the shadow of the baseball cap he wore glanced back at Tree from the driver's seat.

"This the guy?" he asked

Burly guy with a gun nodded. "This is the guy. Meet Samuel Callister."

Tree blanched at this news as the second burly guy squeezed into the passenger seat.

Tree said, "Hold on a minute, what are you talking about?"

The second guy leaned over to the pimply driver and said, "Come on. Let's get going."

"Don't go anywhere," Tree said in an alarmed voice. "There's been a mistake I'm not Scratch Callister."

"You're not?" the second burly guy was straining around to get a better look at Tree. "Then who are you?"

"I'm his bro—his half-brother."

The burly guy with the gun grinned. "You're not a whole brother, huh? Just a half-brother?"

"You're making a mistake," Tree asserted. "I don't know what you want with Scratch, but you've got the wrong guy. I'm Tree Callister. I'm a private detective on Sanibel Island."

That caused Tree's three captors to break into laughter. "That's rich," said the second burly guy. "What the hell would a private detective do on Sanibel Island?"

"For one thing, he might follow his half-brother to a gun show and get mistaken for him."

"Yeah, yeah," the second burly guy said before turning to the pimply driver. "Let's get a move on."

"You're making a mistake," Tree said as the van started forward.

"We don't make mistakes," the second burly guy said.

"Well, that's not quite accurate," the guy with the gun said. "We do make mistakes, but we bury them out in the Everglades."

———————

From his vantage point in the back of the van, Tree could tell little about where they were headed. He gave up trying to explain to his fellow passengers that he was not who they thought he was and started considering that no matter what, an encounter with Scratch always resulted in trouble. If Tree had wondered why they hadn't been in contact for twenty years, this ride in a van with three thugs was a timely reminder.

The end to Tree's protests also ended any need for more conversation. Everyone rode in silence for the better part of an hour.

"Make a right up ahead," ordered the second burly guy.

The pimply driver made a sharp turn that threw Tree hard against the burly guy with the gun knocking the weapon out of his hand and onto his lap. Before anyone else could react, Tree snatched up the gun and held it at the head of the burly guy now without the gun.

"Pull over," Tree said to the driver.

The second burly guy was straining around, showing surprise at what was happening in the rear. "Christ," he said when he saw Tree with the gun. "How the hell did that happen?"

"Pull the van over," Tree repeated.

"What do you think you're doing, Scratch?" The second burly guy was trying to sound calm except he wasn't doing a very good job of it.

"I'm not Scratch and I'm telling you to stop the van."

"What? You're going to shoot three guys? I don't think so."

Tree fired a shot through the front windshield, leaving a neat round hole. The pimply driver yelped in surprise and nearly lost control of his vehicle.

"Pull over!" Tree yelled.

The pimply driver brought the van to a stop.

Tree said to the burly guy without the gun, "Open the door beside you."

The burly guy without the gun hesitated and then turned and pulled at the release latch. The van door slid open. "Okay," Tree said. "Everybody out."

"You're making a mistake," the second burly guy said.

Tree gave the burly guy without the gun a hard shove, thrusting him out of the van. The pimply driver had his door open and was starting to exit.

Tree said to the driver, "Make sure you leave the key in the ignition and the van running."

"Come on, you're not going to take the van are you, Scratch?" whined the pimply driver. "It's my van. I'm still making the goddamn payments."

"Too bad, get out," Tree ordered. The pimply guy swore and then complied.

Tree eased out onto the shoulder of the road as the burly guy without the gun stumbled to his feet. His eyes were on fire with anger.

"I'm going to kill you, you bastard," he declared.

Tree ignored him, keeping his eyes simultaneously on the second burly guy and the pimply driver coming around the front of the van.

When the three were together, trying to look tough and menacing at the same time maintaining awareness that they were facing a man with a gun in a state where you couldn't get into much trouble for shooting the people who had recently abducted you.

"Just out of curiosity," Tree said. "What did Scratch do that would make you decide to kidnap him at a gun show?"

"Don't bullshit us, man," the second burly guy said. "You know what's going down here as well as I do."

"Pretend for a moment I don't have a clue," Tree said.

"You screwed the pooch with the wrong people, amigo. Now you're going to pay the price, if not today, tomorrow—or maybe the next day. Doesn't make a difference to me. But you pay—the devil to pay."

"Keep in mind that you kidnapped the wrong guy," Tree retorted. "When you understand that and finally realize how stupid you are, you might want to think twice before you try anything with Scratch."

Nobody responded. Tree went around and got in the driver's side, slammed the door, shoved the van into forward and shot onto the highway.

12

It had grown dark and had begun to rain as Tree sped along, not certain where he was, driving a van he had stolen, with a gun taken from a trio of toughs who probably didn't like the idea of him taking their gun, once again having walked into a whirlwind of trouble created by a brother—*half*-brother—who historically had caused him nothing but trouble.

He was fumbling in his pocket for his cellphone, intending to call Freddie, when an inky blur leapt into the beam of his headlights. He had a moment to see the bright glow of the panther's eyes before he swung the wheel hard to the right and went skidding off the highway, thinking for another instant that he might be all right just before the van smashed into something and Tree was thrown forward, the world transformed into blurry darkness.

He could hear the beating of the rain on the hood of the van and feel the warmth of blood trickling down the side of his face. He was thinking he had to do something, he couldn't just sit there hung in his seatbelt harness when the driver's-side door opened and a rain-drenched face was caught in the half-light from the van's interior light.

Scratch Callister said, "You okay, brother?"

Tree tried to get the word *half*-brother out of his bloodied mouth. But it wouldn't come.

Scratch reached in and unhooked Tree's seatbelt. "Listen to me, Tremain," he said. "I'm going to lift you out of the van. Are you all right with that?"

When Tree nodded, he went on, "If anything feels broken or you're in pain, let me know. But otherwise, I don't think it's a good idea to hang around here." He grinned. "So to speak."

Tree nodded again and Scratch eased him out into the rain and then steadied him to stand on wobbly legs. He could see the lights of the Porsche drawn up behind the van.

"There's a cut on your forehead and your mouth is bleeding," Scratch noted. "Come on, let's get you back to my car. Okay?"

Tree nodded for a third time.

"Hold on a moment," Scratch said. "I'm going to shut the van down."

Scratch climbed in on the driver's side while Tree leaned against the van, trying to clear his head. He was vaguely aware of the motor being turned off followed by the headlights.

He heard the sound of the van door closing and then Scratch was back taking his arm. "Let's get the hell out of here."

"Were you following me?" Tree demanded once Scratch gunned the Porsche, cranking up the speed, apparently not worried about hitting panthers or anything else. He held a wad of tissues against his bleeding forehead. His mouth still felt bloody from where he had bit his lip slamming forward when the van went off the road.

"Think of me as your guardian angel, old son." Scratch's smile in the greenish light emanating from the dashboard had taken on a Satanic hue. The devil in disguise, Tree couldn't help thinking.

"You're not my guardian anything," Tree said angrily. "You're the devil who keeps getting me into trouble."

"You can't be serious?" Scratch appeared genuinely appalled. "I saved your damned ass back there. What would have happened if I hadn't come along?"

"Because you were following me," Tree insisted.

"Yes, well, old son, who was following whom? I'm outside the gun show headed for my car when I see *you* come out with two scruffy gents who don't look too friendly, you want to know the truth."

"They weren't," Tree interjected.

"There you go. At first, I'm amazed. What would Tremain Callister, not exactly a gun enthusiast despite his unlikely profession, what would he be doing at a gun show? Then the answer occurred to me—Brother Tree is at a gun show because *I* am at a gun show. You followed me there."

"The reason I ended up with those scruffy gents, as you call them, was because they thought I was *you*."

"Me?" Scratch managed to sound convincingly taken aback. "Why would they think you were me?"

"Because they were after you. The question is, *why* were they after you?"

"They couldn't have been after me," Scratch said.

"Yes, they were," Tree said. "They sure as hell weren't after me. What were you doing there, anyway?"

"A couple of business associates. They were at the show," Scratch said in a calmer voice. "I drove out there to meet them."

"What's BlackHeart?"

Scratch took his time about answering. "Why should I know anything about something called BlackHeart?"

"Because that's what was on the banner where your two 'friends' were standing."

"Couldn't say, old son. I wasn't paying any attention to banners." Scratch was back to sounding unconvincing.

"There's also the question of the two thugs who showed up looking for you this morning at the office."

"You're joking," Scratch said. "There must be some mistake. No one's looking for me." He sounded more unconvincing than ever.

"Not even my wife?"

Silence in the Porsche except for the low growl of the motor. "Your wife?"

"Freddie. The woman you love."

"What about her?"

"Why was she visiting you this morning at the Blue Parrot Motel?"

"I have no idea what you're talking about," Scratch said.

"You're lying Scratch, I saw her come out of the motel."

"You'd better talk to Freddie," Scratch said, keeping his eyes on the road as he swung the Porsche onto Daniels Parkway.

"What are you up to, Scratch? What's all this about?"

"Like I said, Tremain, I'm here to help—to help you. As I did tonight by saving your life."

"Scratch, you didn't save my life."

"You know what you are, my good brother. Maybe you don't want to admit it, but you know—you've known since we were kids."

"I don't know what you're talking about, Scratch, and if that's what you think you're blackmailing me about, then you'd better think again."

The twist was back in his smile; the gleam had returned to his eye. "Blackmail, old son? Is that what you think this is?"

"Then what is it? What are you doing back here?"

"Not blackmailing you, that's for certain. Perhaps trying to help you find the destiny you've spent a lifetime ignoring. That could have something to do with it."

"You're crazy," Tree said angrily. "This is all crazy."

"Careful, old son," Scratch said.

"Careful about what?" Tree demanded.

"Careful you don't bleed all over my rental Porsche."

"Go to hell," Tree said.

"The final destination for both of us, old son. The final destination."

By the time Scratch drew up in front of the house on Andy Rosse Lane, Tree was plagued by the thoughts he hated most, the second ones.

"Listen, you'd better stay here tonight," he said to Scratch. "Even though you insist no one's after you, someone is."

"I'll be all right," Scratch said.

"If I can find you, others can, too. You're welcome to stay the night."

"I appreciate that, bro, but I've got a few things to take care of."

"Anything to do with that bag?" Tree asked.

Instantly, the built-in merriment on Scratch's face was gone, replaced by a shadow of suspicion. "What bag?"

"The one they gave you at the gun show. Is that why those guys were after you?"

"I keep telling you. No one's after me."

"Then what was the bag for?"

"Please quickly understand what's good for you, old son," Scratch said, quiet menace edging the strained nonchalance in his voice. "Forget you ever asked that question. Whatever you think you saw, you didn't see. Do you understand me? You didn't see anything."

Tree looked at him in astonishment. "What's wrong with you, anyway?"

"I'm tired; it's been a long day," Scratch snapped. "I saved your behind. Exhausting work. Let's leave it at that."

Tree gritted his teeth and got out of the Porsche. Before he closed the door, he said to Scratch, "Incidentally, what did you do with the gun?"

"What gun?" Scratch gave him a blank look.

13

For perhaps the ten millionth time since they had married, Freddie applied Neosporin antibiotic ointment to the cuts on Tree's forehead and face. "I should buy this stuff by the gallon," she said grimly.

"It's worse than it looks," Tree said, flinching as she applied the ointment.

"You're a big baby," Freddie said. "You're not built for detective work. Too low a pain threshold."

"Tell me about it," Tree said.

While Freddie administered to his wounds, Tree explained what had happened, leaving out the part where he had seen her at the Blue Parrot Motel.

"I guess I'd better tell you," she said when he finished.

"Tell me what?"

"I was going to tell you when you came in, except that you were bleeding, a not uncommon state of affairs in our marriage when you arrive home. Thus, I was distracted."

"What were you going to tell me?"

"That I was at the Blue Parrot this morning."

"I know you were," Tree said.

"I know you know," Freddie said.

"How would you know that?"

"I saw you in that truck," said Freddie.

"You saw me in the truck?" Tree couldn't believe it.

"You think you're so clever."

"That's the problem," Tree said. "I think I'm clever and then I constantly end up being reminded that I'm not clever at all—particularly when it comes to any attempt to fool you."

"I don't fool easily," Freddie confirmed.

"That's for sure," Tree said.

"I didn't know what you were doing in a truck in the parking lot at the Blue Parrot Motel but I did see you."

"Why didn't you say something?"

"I wanted to see if *you* said something."

"I didn't think you saw me," Tree said.

"What difference does that make?"

"It does beg the question," Tree said.

"What kind of question does it beg?"

"The question of what you were doing at the Blue Parrot in the first place."

"I was meeting with your brother," Freddie said.

"Half-brother," Tree said.

"Among the subjects we discussed was the fact that he is your brother and not your half-brother."

"That's crazy," Tree said.

"Scratch says there is what you were told, therefore what you believe, and then there is the truth."

"Which is?"

"That he is your brother."

"That's why you went to the motel? To find out whether Scratch is my brother or my half-brother?"

"No, of course not." Freddie showed a trace of irritation. "I went to the motel because he phoned me and asked me to meet him."

"Why did he do that?"

"He said he had something important to tell me."

"Did he?"

Freddie shrugged. "The deep dark secret in your past that I don't know about."

"And he told you what it is?"

"No, he said you would have to tell me. But he wanted me to know that he had taken an oath with himself to
protect your secret."

"I don't know how much of an oath he's taken," Tree
said. "I think it depends on how much he can get out of
me."

"Are you sure you're not being a trifle cynical?"

"I think the better word where Scratch is concerned is
'realistic.' I'm not sure why he is here or what he's done to
encourage the animosity of pissed-off men with guns, but
I believe it involves this BlackHeart organization, whatever
that is. And it almost certainly involves money that he has
taken from people who are not happy about giving it to
him."

"And where do you fit into this scenario?"

"Depending on what happens, I believe he wants money from me in return for his silence."

"You actually believe your own brother is blackmailing
you?"

"Half-brother. No matter what he tells you. And yes,
I certainly think he will try that if he has to. Given what
unfolded today, he must be in trouble. He says he isn't, but
as usual, Scratch is lying."

"The people who are after him," Freddie said.

"What about them?"

"They're not after Scratch. They're after you. They think
you're Scratch."

"Despite my best efforts to assure them I'm not."

"Keep in mind that whether you like it or not, you're
in trouble, too."

"Whenever Scratch shows up, that's what happens. He
may be in trouble. But by the time he's finished, I'm in
even bigger trouble."

Freddie sighed deeply as she replaced the cap on the Neosporin. "That's it, the nurse is off duty having done the best she can to tend to the battlefield wounded."

"I've decided to desert and run away with you," Tree said, taking her hand. "It's a farewell to arms."

"Yeah, right," Freddie said. "Let's get some sleep, Lieutenant Henry, and hope against hope you don't get into any more shit tonight."

————

By the time Tree settled in bed beside Freddie, his whole body was aching. Each time he closed his eyes, the black panther came charging out of the darkness.

He jerked upright. Freddie, with her back to him, issued soft snores. Relieved that he had not awakened her, Tree slipped out of bed and went into the den and settled in front of his computer screen.

He lingered for a time trying to decide if he was tired enough to go back to bed and this time fall asleep. He decided he was too keyed up. He brought up the Google search engine on his screen and typed in BlackHeart. That produced a lot of references to, literally, a black heart: "Across many cultures, humans have long believed the *heart* governed emotion, thought, and character—and was even the seat of the soul itself," read one explanation.

"The color *black*, meanwhile, has ancient associations with evil, evoking darkness, storms, decay, and death. In Old English, we can find both *heart* used for a person's emotional and moral center and *black* characterizing something as 'wicked.' *Black-hearted*, or 'malevolent,' doesn't appear until at least the 1630s. A *black heart*, specifically, emerges in records by the 1700s and 1800s, often appearing in literary contexts to describe a melancholy, hateful person with evil intentions."

Was Scratch "a melancholy, hateful person with evil intentions?"

He could be, Tree decided. He certainly could be.

He scrolled down until he came across BlackHeart.com and brought the website up on the screen. There was the familiar logo, a black heart with a lightning bolt slicing through it. Beneath the logo were the words: Confusion. Confrontation. Disruption.

Further down the homepage, a photograph of the two men Tree had seen with Scratch at the gun show. They were identified as Custer and Armstrong Duckett. "Our benefactors," according to the website.

But no more information than that.

When Tree hit the About Us tab on the menu the same three words were repeated: Confusion. Confrontation. Disruption. They were repeated again under Our Mission Statement.

Tree was about to leave the site when he noticed one more tab: Watcher. He clicked his mouse on the tab and up came a blurry black-and-white photograph of a tall man with a shade of beard, hands on his hips in front of a stand of palm trees. It was hard to tell from the photo, but the man looked an awful lot like Lobo Salvador.

It couldn't be, Tree thought. It couldn't possibly be the man he had encountered by a campfire late at night on the side of a Florida highway, the first time he swerved to miss hitting a panther.

He peered closely at the photograph to assure himself that the Watcher wasn't Lobo Salvador.

But it was.

14

The next morning, Tree's body, crying out for revenge at being battered yet again the day before, fired shards of pain through him so that he could barely squeeze into Freddie's Mercedes.

"Serves you right," Freddie said as she drove down Captiva Drive.

"It was either me or the panther," Tree said.

"Sorry, but I find it very hard to swallow the notion that you twice drove off the road because of a panther."

"I'm the Panther King, what can I tell you?" Tree said.

"Either that or you're getting too old to drive a car."

"It was a van," Tree countered. "Which reminds me, somehow I've got to get out to North Fort Myers to pick up Gladys' truck."

Freddie shot him a sideways glance as they approached Blind Pass. "Who's Gladys?"

"I forgot all about it given everything that went on yesterday," Tree said. "Rex has decided we need a receptionist at the office."

"I don't believe it," Freddie said. "The two of you may need to have your heads read, as my mother used to say, but you don't need a receptionist."

"Rex believes his memoir will be a huge international bestseller and he's going to need someone like Gladys Demchuk to help him manage all the attention."

"And what is it about Gladys that attracts Rex?"

"For one thing, she has a gun," Tree said.

"Rex needs a woman with a gun?"

"Well, she managed to put the gun to good use a few minutes into her first day on the job. I guess that says something about her value."

"But what's she doing coming to work with a gun?" Freddie sounded incredulous, incredulousness being a recurring theme in their marriage.

"Gladys used to be a private detective in Los Angeles. That's where I met her, although back then she was known as Blue Streak. I believe I told you about her."

"The woman who used to be a porn actress?"

"Adult film star is the way I believe Blue prefers to refer to herself."

"I see. Excuse me."

"But that part of her life was over a long time ago. Gladys was just a kid back then. She's been through a lot of changes, including ending her career as a detective in California. Now she's here in Southwest Florida and is back to her original name."

"Gladys Demchuk."

"That's right."

"Not exactly a porn star's name."

"Like I said, adult film actress, if you're talking about that period of her life."

"Sorry, I'm not up on the current porn vernacular."

"I'm here to help," Tree said.

"I'm repeating myself, but I still don't think you need a receptionist," Freddie said as she turned onto Periwinkle Way.

"Take it up with Rex," Tree said.

"You guys," Freddie said. "Honestly."

———

"Freddie doesn't think we need a receptionist," Tree said to Rex when he got to the office.

"Freddie should have been here yesterday about the time those two thugs were on the verge of beating the crap out of you," Rex said mildly.

"There is that," Tree admitted.

"I need a receptionist," Rex said. "*You* need a guardian angel."

Gladys chose that moment to appear in the office. "Sorry I'm late," she said. "I had to wait for the guy I picked up in a bar last night to give me a ride."

Rex regarded her with surprise. "You picked up a guy in a bar?"

"I let him think he picked me up," Gladys said, dropping her shoulder bag on her desk. "But actually, it was the other way around. But then that's the way it is, isn't it? It's always the other way around."

"I was just saying to Tree that he needs a guardian angel," Rex said.

"I thought I was being hired as a receptionist," Gladys said.

"We may have to change your job description," Rex said.

"Along with danger pay."

"For this job or for last night?" Rex asked.

"The guy I picked up was the one in danger," Gladys said. "I was fine." She addressed Tree. "I had to let him stay overnight because without my truck, I needed a ride this morning. I didn't see it outside."

"We're going to have to drive out to the Lee Civic Center," Tree said.

"What's it doing out there?" Rex asked.

"It's a long story," Tree said.

"It always is," Rex said, rolling his eyes. "It always is."

The vast Lee Civic Center parking lot was empty except for a single vehicle—the burned-out husk of Gladys' pick-up truck. It was cordoned off with fluttery yellow police tape so that Gladys, Tree, and Rex could only stand nearby inspecting the wreckage.

"This is turning out to be quite a job," Gladys observed. "Day One I'm waving a gun at two hoods and then my truck gets torched at a gun show."

"I tried to warn you," Rex said.

"I really liked that old truck," Gladys said sadly. "That old truck got me from California to Florida. We had a lot of adventures together."

"I'm really sorry, Gladys," Tree said. "It's my half-brother. He's nothing but trouble."

"Tree," Gladys said, turning to him. "It's you. *You're* nothing but trouble." Almost immediately, she had second thoughts. "As a new employee, I probably shouldn't have said that."

"We encourage all members of the staff to speak their minds," Rex said.

"No, we don't," Tree said.

"Here's what we're going to do," Rex said. "I'm going to take Tree back to the office. Then Gladys and I are going to see Bad Boy Billy Boyd who owns a truck dealership on Tamiami Trail, and he's going to offer Gladys a great deal on a new truck, that—" and here he gave Tree the eye—"you and I will pay for. Any objections?"

Tree swallowed before he said, "None that I can think of."

Rex looked at Gladys. "You're going to have to deal with the police at some point."

"I wonder about that," Gladys said.

"They'll get your registration from the license plates," Rex said.

"Except the license plates on the truck…" Gladys allowed her voice to trail off.

"What about them?"

"They're not exactly mine," Gladys said.

Tree and Rex traded glances. "Ah, Gladys, Gladys," Rex said. "Still walking on the wild side."

"I wouldn't say I walk there," Gladys countered. "It's more accurate to say I occasionally lose my way and find myself in that location."

"Where no license and registration are required," Tree said.

"Let's say it's possible to get by without them," Gladys said.

"Let's just get the hell out of here," Rex said.

15

The individual waiting in the office when Tree arrived back at the Cattle Dock Bait Company was African American.

Thin to the point of skinny, smartly dressed in white jeans and a loose pullover, he wore a thin gold chain around his neck and on his fingers lots of silver matching the silver bracelets on his wrists.

"I'm not certain I am in the correct place," he said when Tree entered.

"It depends," Tree said. "If you are looking for bait you are in the wrong section of the right place. If you are looking for a private investigator then you are in the right place."

"I am not looking for bait," said the African-American gentleman. "I am not a fisherperson. I am waiting for Mr. Tree Callister."

"I'm Tree Callister."

"I am Albert Aberfoyle," he stated formally. He did not stand as he shook Tree's hand. "You head the Sanibel Sunset Detective Agency, am I correct about that?"

"That's right. What can I do for you, Mr. Aberfoyle?"

"I am on a quest, sir," he explained. "I have come from Atlanta, via Detroit, and Toronto in Canada, in pursuit of that quest. Now I am here, and am seeking local help so that I may finally bring my quest to an end."

"And what kind of quest is that, Mr. Aberfoyle?"

"It is the quest to find the man who ruined the life of my daughter and caused her untimely suicide. It is my ambition to find this man and bring him to justice. I have chased him across much of America. My latest information is that he is somewhere here in Southwest Florida. I am unfamiliar with this area and therefore am seeking local help, someone who knows the terrain, so to speak. I am hoping you might be that person."

Tree groaned inwardly thinking that *damn*, after thirteen years in Florida, the local terrain remained among the many, many things he didn't know much about.

"Can I ask what happened that your daughter took her life?"

"This man, sir, is a con man, a devil if you will. He filled my daughter full of false hope. She had gone through an ugly divorce, had one wing down when this terrible man happened along. He claimed he had special powers, that he could make her life better. All she had to do was sign a contract with him and her life would improve."

"And did it?"

"I suppose it did for a time, at least it did according to my daughter. But then this man began to extract the stipulations laid out in the contract, thousands of dollars she had to pay out to him. He was ruthless, unremitting in taking her money, and when it was all gone, he disappeared, as if in a puff of smoke. My daughter was broken financially and heartbroken emotionally. It was all too much for her. That's when she took her life."

"I'm sorry, Mr. Aberfoyle," Tree said. "It sounds as though you've been through a bad time, and you have all my sympathy, you really do."

"I appreciate that, Mr. Callister. But as you can imagine, at this point I do not need sympathy, I need help."

"And you're sure this man is in Southwest Florida?"

"In the Fort Myers area. That is my information, yes. Will you help me?"

Silently, Tree wondered how he could do that. It would be like looking for a needle in a haystack, and Tree was ill-equipped for finding needles in haystacks. Aloud, he said, "I can't make any promises, but I will see what I can do."

"That would be much appreciated," Aberfoyle said.

"Do you have any idea where he might be staying?"

"Unfortunately, no."

"But you must have a name."

"It's a name I am loathe to speak. It turns my stomach each time I am forced to repeat it."

"A name will certainly help me," Tree said.

"Yes, of course. His name is Chamuco. Carl Chamuco."

Tree started when he heard the name. "Chamuco," he repeated.

"You know it?" Aberfoyle asked.

"It's Spanish," Tree said.

"Yes, I believe it is."

"It means devil, doesn't it?"

"I didn't know that," Aberfoyle said. "But given this man's behavior, I cannot be surprised."

"Is he Spanish?"

"Not as far as I know."

"Do you have anything else I can use. A photograph?"

"In retrospect, it's understandable, but he refused to have his photograph taken when he was with my daughter. He went to great lengths to prevent this. He said photographs robbed him of his soul—of his power to help those less fortunate than himself. That is what the bastard said."

"That's unfortunate," Tree said.

"However, I do have one picture." Aberfoyle opened his cellphone and used his thumb to scroll through a series of photos until he found the one he was looking for. He handed the phone to Tree. "That's Chamuco in the background. Not very good I'm afraid."

Tree studied the photo on the phone. In the foreground, Aberfoyle smiled with an attractive woman in her thirties. Behind her, Tree could see another figure, somewhat out of focus, a man who wasn't smiling.

A man who looked an awful lot like Scratch Callister.

"Is something wrong?" Albert Aberfoyle asked.

Tree shook himself out of his reverie. "It's not much of a photo, but please send it to me via my email and I'll do the best I can."

Albert Aberfoyle looked at him with freshly suspicious eyes. "You look as though you have seen a ghost."

"Saddened to see a photograph of your daughter," Tree said quickly. "She was a lovely young woman."

"It is the tragedy of my life," Aberfoyle said.

"I can imagine," Tree said.

"We should discuss your fee." Before Tree could reply, Aberfoyle reached into the leather satchel he was carrying and brought out a thick envelope and plunked it down on the desk.

"There is seven thousand dollars," he said. "That should get you started."

"Cash?"

"You have something against cash?"

"Tree looked at the money and then turned his gaze back to Aberfoyle. "What do you do for a living, Mr. Aberfoyle?"

"You are suspicious of clients with cash?"

"Frankly, yes," Tree said.

"The money speaks for itself," Aberfoyle said.

Tree looked at the money and then said, "Where can I get in touch with you?"

Aberfoyle produced a card and wrote out a number on the back.

"My local cellphone number. Please keep in touch and let me know as soon as you find out anything."

"These other places where you looked for Carl Chamuco, did you hire local investigators?"

"I did," Aberfoyle said. "But they weren't much help." He stood and for the first time allowed something resembling a smile. "I am praying you will be different, Mr. Callister."

Tree wasn't certain prayers were going to be of much help.

———

After Albert Aberfoyle had left, Tree stared some more at the envelope full of money, wondering again about the kind of client who dropped seven thousand dollars in cash on his desk without batting an eye, lamenting the weakness in his DNA that continually allowed him to be drawn into suspicious situations, particularly when they involved Scratch Callister, consoling himself that it was his half-brother and therefore he had no choice but to get involved.

At least that's what he kept telling himself as he unlocked the bottom drawer of his desk and dropped the money inside.

He telephoned Freddie and although she grumbled a bit—"It's time you replaced your Volkswagen Beetle and stopped relying on me"—agreed to drive to the office and pick him up.

Once he was beside her in the Mercedes, he directed her back onto the causeway as he told of his latest client, and the blurry background photograph of the man Albert Aberfoyle believed had brought about his daughter's death.

"Aberfoyle says his name is Carl Chamuco, but the guy in the photo looks an awful lot like Scratch."

"But you can't say for certain it's Scratch," Freddie said as she came off the causeway and turned onto Periwinkle Way.

"Not for certain, but the guy in the photo bears a resemblance to Scratch, let's put it that way. Aberfoyle is supposed to send me the photo so you can have a look for yourself." As he spoke Tree checked his email. "He hasn't done it yet."

"But maybe it's not Scratch," Freddie said.

"When I saw the photograph, I didn't immediately think, gee, that can't possibly be Scratch. The first thing I thought when I saw it was, shit, that looks like Scratch."

Tree put his phone away. "There's something else. Something scary."

"What's that?"

"It's the name of the guy Aberfoyle is looking for."

"You said Carl Chamuco."

"Exactly. Carl Chamuco."

Freddie knit her brow. "I don't get it."

"Chamuco is Spanish for devil. That guy I met after I ran off the road. Lobo Salvador? Like I told you, he warned me about a chamuco. A devil. I would meet a chamuco and I had better be careful—*Que dios te ayude*, he said."

"God help you," Freddie translated.

"Exactly," Tree said.

The traffic on Periwinkle at this time of day was moving pretty well. Freddie stopped the Mercedes to allow a couple of bike riders to cross the road.

"This goes back to the idea that your brother is the devil, does it not?" Freddie asked when she started forward.

"Half-brother," Tree said. "And it's a possibility that keeps coming up."

"Because he was hit by lightning as a kid? That makes him the devil?"

"I think it convinced Scratch," Tree said.

"Tree, I'll remind you again: there is no such thing as the devil."

Tree didn't say anything.

"Tree?" Freddie said.

He glanced over at her.

"Repeat after me: there is no such thing as the devil."

"There's no such thing as the devil." Tree paused. "But if there is, he's my brother."

"Your half-brother," Freddie corrected. "And he's not the devil."

"He may not be a devil," Tree said. "But he is a con man and probably the guy Aberfoyle is looking for."

"And what are you going to do if he is?"

Tree hesitated before he said, "That's a good question."

"Then why don't you try answering it?"

"Because I don't have an answer," Tree said.

"I thought so," Freddie said.

16

There was no one at the Blue Parrot Motel registered under the name of Samuel Callister. Nor was there anyone called Scratch Callister.

"What about Carl Chamuco?" Tree asked.

"Nope, no one by that name either." The ancient desk clerk looked bemused. "How many names does this dude have, anyway?"

Tree turned to Freddie. "Do you remember what room he was in?"

Freddie shook her head. "He was outside in the parking lot when I got here."

Tree returned to the ancient desk clerk. "This guy was driving a Porsche," Tree said.

"Oh, *that* guy," said the desk clerk. "Why didn't you say so in the first place. Likable dude. Patrick Diavolo."

"That's the name he gave you?"

"The name on the license he showed me, yessir. Name on his American Express card, too."

"What room is he in?" Tree asked.

"Ain't no one in the room," the desk clerk said.

"What do you mean?"

"Patrick checked out early this morning."

"Any idea where he went?"

The desk clerk smiled and shook his head. "You're like me, fella. You read too many of them private detective novels where the guy the shamus is after leaves a forwarding address. No one does that anymore. Fella checks out now, and he's gone. Who knows where?"

"Okay," Tree said. "Thanks."

"He did say something about a brother here on the island."

Half-brother," Tree said.

"Maybe he went to stay with him."

———————

What looked like a new Ford Ranger truck was parked outside the Cattle Dock Bait Company when Freddie dropped Tree off.

Inside, Tree half expected to find Scratch waiting for him, that trademark smirk on his face. At least a trademark for Tree, who had, in his estimation at least, spent a lifetime enduring it. Not to mention that goddamn twinkle in his eye.

But Scratch, thankfully, was not in the office. Instead, Rex pounded away at his laptop while Gladys busied herself filing her nails. Not the best use of her time, Tree surmised. She looked up as he entered and gave him a smile. Rex continued to be preoccupied at his laptop.

"Don't tell me that truck out there is yours," Tree said to Gladys.

Her smile widened. She had stopped filing her nails. "I love this job. I'm here a day and I've got a new truck."

"The previously driven 2019 Ford Ranger SuperCrew." Rex looked up from his laptop. "That's because you burned down her other truck."

"I didn't burn down her truck," Tree protested.

"Nonetheless, you're responsible. Ergo, Gladys has a previously-driven truck. With proper license and registration, I might add."

"Rex is trying to make an honest woman out of me," Gladys said.

"It's a process," Rex said.

"How much was the truck?' asked Tree.

"My old pal Bad Boy Billy Boyd gave me a great price."

"Yeah? What great price did good old Bad Boy Billy give you?"

"Fifteen thousand with a few bells and whistles thrown in."

Tree closed his eyes briefly before staggering over to his desk.

"But you don't have to pay me back right away," Rex added.

"What about Gladys' insurance?"

"What insurance?" Gladys said.

"We're getting her insurance," Rex affirmed to Tree. "Don't worry."

"In L.A. they think you're a pussy if you have auto insurance."

"You're not exactly out of place here, either," Rex said. "But I need you in the office, not in jail."

Tree opened his desk drawer and pulled out the envelope Albert Aberfoyle had left him. He threw it to Rex who caught it adroitly. "What's this?"

"A down payment."

Gladys resumed filing her nails.

Tree's phone rang. Gladys stopped filing her nails. "Let me get it," she said. "Sanibel Sunset Detective Agency."

Tree had to admit Gladys sounded impressively authoritative as if the caller had reached a real, functioning office. Worth the fifteen thousand right there, Tree thought.

"Who shall I say is calling?"

Gladys covered the phone with her hand and said to Tree, "A Mister Duckett on line two."

There was no line two. Nonetheless, Tree picked up the receiver. "Mr. Callister, hold please," a pleasant male baritone said. "I have Mr. Custer Duckett for you."

The line went dead for a minute and then another male voice, this one deep and southern said, "Mr. Cannister?"

"It's Callister," Tree said. "Tree Callister."

"Sorry about that Mr. Callister," the voice said. "Can't read my assistant's writing."

"What can I do for you, Mr. Duckett?"

"Well, sir, I think it's high time we got together, don't you?"

"I don't know," Tree said. "Is it?"

"I certainly think it is and so does my brother, Armstrong. We're what they call Irish twins. Have you heard that phrase before, Mr. Calendar? Irish twins?"

"Callister. You and your brother were born within the same year."

"Sorry about that. Yes, Callister it is. And you're right. Good for you. My kid brother," he said, adding the sort of staged laugh that indicated he had told this little joke many times before.

"BlackHeart," Tree said.

"Why, yes, that's it exactly." Custer Duckett sounded surprised. "Confusion. Confrontation. Disruption. That's us. Your brother Samuel has recommended you."

"Half-brother," Tree said.

"Mr. Callister, we have some work that requires a man of your particular talents."

"I'm not sure I have particular talents," Tree said.

"I'm willing to bet you're being modest, but let's find out about that. Armstrong and I, we're out here adjacent to Lovers Key on Fort Myers Beach. How be you drive out so we can have a talk, kind of size each other up?"

"You don't know where I can find Samuel, by any chance?"

Custer Duckett chuckled. "You don't know where your own brother is, doesn't say much about your private investigative abilities, now does it?"

"Like I said, half-brother. I haven't heard from Samuel for a while. I thought maybe you'd been in touch with him."

"In fact, your, as you say, half-brother, is along the lines of what we'd like to discuss with you. Why don't we say tomorrow morning around 11 o'clock?

"You say Lovers Key?"

"Well, don't tell anyone, but we're actually on Black Island, adjacent to Lovers Key."

"Black Island?"

"You find that ironic?" Custer asked.

"Should I?"

"Palm Tree Lane. Number thirty-three. You shouldn't have too much trouble finding us. After all, you are a detective, aren't you?"

Before Tree had a chance to deny that allegation, Custer Duckett, with a final chuckle, hung up.

17

When you think you can't possibly drive further out Estero Boulevard on Fort Myers Beach, and when you are well past the Santini Mall, that's when you start to get close to Lovers Key and Black Island. They are among the countless barrier islands along the coast, joined to Fort Myers Beach by a causeway.

Most people who are familiar with the key know it's a state park where you can walk on the beach, swim, fish, kayak, all the things one does at Florida state parks.

What most people don't know, Tree mused as he crossed the causeway onto the key, is that a lot of rich people live out here.

Apparently, the Duckett brothers were rich people.

He turned off Estero Boulevard onto Black Island and travelled along a narrow roadway, thick with foliage on either side to hide the walls that hid the very rich people who lived along here from the prying eyes of those less blessed.

The Palm Tree Lane address Custer Duckett had given him was at the end of the road. If you tried to go further, you drove into the high stone wall that protected the Ducketts from the world. The wall was obscured by clinging magenta bougainvillea in full bloom.

Tree parked close to the discreet entranceway protected by a wrought iron gate built into the wall. He announced himself on the intercom. That produced silence from inside, allowing Tree to consider that he had spent much of his life waiting to be admitted into the lives of rich people, never with very satisfactory results. He had little reason to believe today would be any different.

A buzzing sound warned that the gate was about to open. He pushed through into an impressive garden intersected by a flagstone pathway. The two burly guys Tree had encountered at the gun show stood on the path, blocking his way. Today, they wore baseball caps and cargo shorts. If they didn't look so dangerous, they would look ridiculous, Tree reflected. He thought it best not to point this out to the two burly guys.

"Good to see the two of you," Tree said. "How've you been? Did you get your van back all right?"

In response, their faces shaded beneath the peaks of their baseball caps, the two gave him identical bleak looks. "I'm looking for my gun," said the burly guy who had dropped the gun in his lap.

"You know what?" Tree said. "I think it's better for you if you don't have a gun."

"The Ducketts are waiting for you on the beach," the other burly guy who didn't have a gun said. "I'll take you down there."

Tree followed him through the garden, out another gate to a windy expanse of beach, deserted except for two figures jumping around in the water. The Duckett brothers at play, Tree surmised.

"You wait on the beach," ordered the burly guy.

Tree walked across the sand to a pair of orange Tommy Bahama beach chairs arranged beneath umbrellas. Tree stood under one of the umbrellas watching the hazy figures frolic in the water. Eventually one of the figures saw him and waved.

The two Ducketts took on solid shape as they emerged from the water, tanned, in matching Speedo swimsuits, fit considering both men must be in their late sixties. The totally bald, slightly taller and better built of the two, stuck out his hand and said, "Custer Duckett, Mr. Collister. We spoke on the phone."

"Callister," Tree said.

"Jesus wept, I knew that. Callister."

Tree shook the hand of the slightly shorter and less-lean Duckett who marked the difference between himself and his brother with a trimmed mustache. "Armstrong Duckett, Mr. Callister. Any trouble finding the place? We're sort of isolated down here."

"No problem," Tree said. "And even better, my two pals from the other day at the gun show were at the door to greet me."

The two brothers stared at Tree as though he was an interesting specimen in a Petri dish. Finally, Custer Duckett said, "You look like you're about to melt, Mr. Callister. How be we get out of the sun? I think they've got lunch ready for us on the terrace."

"Hope you brought your appetite with you," Armstrong Duckett added.

Tree followed the two Speedo-clad brothers along a wooden walkway up onto a terrace where a dining table had been set out with a white linen cloth and place settings for three, the silverware gleaming in the sunlight.

"Take a seat," Armstrong said.

As soon as they were settled, waiters in white waistcoats appeared with large bowls. "Our chef, Miguel, does a wonderful gazpacho." Custer related this news in a conspiratorial voice as though he didn't want it to get out.

Armstrong smiled knowingly when he added, "Just so you know, Miguel won't reveal his recipe."

"I'll keep that in mind," Tree said, picking up a soup-spoon and dipping it into the gazpacho.

"Cold soup on a hot day," Custer said. "Just what the doctor ordered."

Tree swallowed a spoonful of the gazpacho. It tasted like…well, gazpacho. Tomatoey with a little bite. Gazpacho.

Aloud he said, "Delicious."

"Remember," admonished Custer. "Our Miguel won't give you the recipe."

"Darn," Tree said.

The two brothers laughed heartily and then dug into their soup. Armstrong dropped his spoon. "It's not that good," he announced.

"It's fine," countered Custer. "It's Miguel's gazpacho."

"Fine isn't good enough. And this isn't even fine."

"It's great," Custer said, an edge to his voice. "Quit complaining about it."

"Don't tell me to quit complaining, as you say." Armstrong glared at his brother. That reduced them both to silence. They made noises consuming their gazpacho.

Finally, Armstrong mumbled, "I wasn't complaining."

"You were complaining," Custer asserted. "You are always complaining."

"With you around, there's plenty to complain about," Armstrong said.

Armstrong was right. The gazpacho wasn't that great. Out loud Tree said, "Maybe we should get past these gazpacho discussions and talk about what it is you called me here for."

Armstrong looked at Tree as though he should know full well why they called him. "Didn't Custer tell you?"

"Tell me what?"

Armstrong glared at his brother. "You were *supposed* to tell him."

"There was an unfortunate case of mistaken identity the other day at the gun show."

"What kind of case?" demanded Armstrong.

"A case where Lenny and Bob thought Mr. Callister here was his brother, Samuel."

"Half-brother," Tree said.

"By the time the situation got itself ironed out," Custer went on, "I wasn't able to properly brief him."

"And when were you going to inform me of all this?"

"It wasn't necessary, was it? A simple phone call was all it took for Mr. Callahan to join us."

"Callister," Tree said. "Incidentally, did either of you put Lenny and Bob up to torching the truck I left in the parking lot at the gun show?"

Custer and Armstrong traded hot looks. "You must have a talk with Lenny and Bob," Custer said. "They're out of control. They must be reprimanded in the strongest possible terms."

"They're very good at what they do," Armstrong offered.

"Their behavior is unacceptable," Custer pronounced.

"You might also consider reimbursing my receptionist. It was her truck they torched."

"We will see to it," Custer said.

"All this and shitty gazpacho, too," Armstrong said. "It's a wonder Mr. Callister even showed up today."

"The fish course will be much better," promised Custer.

Tree said, "We're still not getting down to why I'm here, other than to listen to the two of you squabble."

"Are we squabbling?" Custer raised his eyebrows in surprise. "I don't think we're *squabbling*, as you put it. My brother and I get along perfectly well."

"I'm not sure I would use the word 'perfect,' in describing our relationship," Armstrong said.

That caused both men to chuckle. "You probably have a point," acknowledged Custer.

They chuckled some more.

"It was our father who made all the money, of course," Custer went on. "Tons of the stuff. Hedge fund nonsense, I don't understand but thank goodness he did. Armstrong is just like Father. That's why we get along if not quite perfectly some days. He knows money. I know how to spend it."

They both laughed. "It was Father who named us after General George Armstrong Custer," Armstrong said, wiping at his eyes. "The great American Indian fighter."

"Not so great, as it turned out," Custer said. "And these days it is correct to say, First Nations fighter."

"Doesn't have much of a ring to it," Armstrong said.

"Nonetheless."

Armstrong dropped his spoon and sat back, contemplatively. "Evka, now there's a subject neither one of us knows anything about," he said.

"Women," Custer added. "Unknowable territory."

"If it's any consolation," Armstrong said, "Father knew nothing about women either—and he married six of them. Was no wiser at the end—as he admitted himself."

"Still confused even on his death bed," Custer agreed. "The two of us can take some consolation from the fact that we only got it wrong once." Custer said.

"But boy, did we ever," Armstrong said.

Tree was beginning to think they had forgotten he was sitting there. "I'm sorry," he interrupted. "I'm losing the thread here. Who is Evka?"

"Evka Bermann," Armstrong explained. "Czech, if nationality matters. My wife."

"But she was mine first," Custer said.

Tree looked at the two brothers in astonishment. "You were both married to the same woman?"

"Evka, yes," Armstrong confirmed. "At different times, of course."

"I see," Tree said.

"I married Evka," Custer said, "and then the next thing I know, she's having an affair with my brother."

"It wasn't an *affair*, as such," Armstrong protested.

"What would you call it then?" demanded Custer.

"A little light fooling around is all," Armstrong said.

"But you married her," Custer countered.

"Water under the bridge as it turns out," Armstrong said with a sigh. "So much water under the bridge."

Custer turned his attention to Tree. "Which brings us to the reason why we invited you today."

"Finally," said Tree.

"We want you to find Evka," Custer said.

"She's gone?" Tree was struggling to get his head around all this.

"Simply disappeared," said Armstrong.

"She hasn't *disappeared*," Custer interjected. "Like I've told you repeatedly—"

"Reminded me far too much," grumbled Armstrong.

"She's run off with that no-good son of a bitch."

"We don't know that for certain," Armstrong said. "That's where our friend Mr. Collins comes into the picture."

"Callister," Tree said. "What are you saying? She's with someone else?"

"That's what we're suspecting, all right," Custer said.

"Do you know who this person is?"

Now both brothers regarded him with disbelief. Armstrong found his voice first, "Why, with your brother."

"You mean Scratch—Samuel?"

"We know him better as Patrick Diavolo," Armstrong said. "A devil, if there ever was one."

"Patrick Diavolo?"

"That's the name he was using, yes."

"But I just saw you with him at the gun show," Tree said. "You gave him a bag."

"Full of money," Custer said. "The money he demanded so that he would leave Evka alone."

"Except we don't believe he has left her alone," Armstrong said. "That's where you come in, Mister—"

"Please, call me Tree."

"That's where you come in, Tree. We want you to ascertain whether or not that devil is with Evka and report back to us."

"This must be done with utmost discretion, of course," Custer added. "The last thing we want is for Evka to find out we are prying into her life."

"But she should not be with this man," Armstrong said.

"You do realize that this is my half-brother."

"All the more reason to hire you," Custer said. "You know Samuel. You can get to him, find out the truth. We suspect he's taken us for a ride and I can tell you, Tree, we do not like being taken for a ride."

"How much did you pay him?"

Neither brother said anything. "How much?" Tree repeated.

Custer swallowed hard, seeming to have difficulty getting the words out. "Three million dollars," he said, practically choking.

"In cash, in that bag," Armstrong added.

"I can't believe it," Tree said. "You simply handed over three million dollars to Scratch—in *cash*?"

Rather than answer, Armstrong reached down beside his chair for a leather valise Tree hadn't noticed before. He placed the valise on the table, unzipped it and pulled out 8X10 photographs. "My wife, Evka," Armstrong said, presenting the photos to Tree as if they were evidence.

"My former wife," Custer added.

Tree looked down at the photos. Evka was blonde and wearing a two-piece bathing suit that did little to hide the reasons the Ducketts were probably interested in her in the first place. She smiled alluringly into the camera. Was that a three-million-dollar smile? Apparently, it was.

"That's part of what we want you to do," Custer said. "If Evka is with him, you must do your best to get our money back."

"Along with Evka," Armstrong added.

"I don't think you ever intended to let Scratch keep the money, did you?" Tree suggested.

The brothers gave him identical quizzical looks. "I'm afraid I don't understand what you're getting at," Custer said.

"When your two goons, Lenny and Bob, mistook me for Scratch and shoved me into their van, the plan was to take back the three million. But Lenny and Bob screwed up and Scratch got away with the money—and maybe Evka, as well."

Custer looked around and his face brightened. "Ah, here we go. The fish course."

The white-coated waiters swept in again, this time bearing plates of salmon.

"Miguel does it in a spice rub with a mango salsa," Armstrong said as a plate was placed on the table in front of Tree.

Custer placed his hand gently on Tree's arm. "Find Evka and bring our money back, and do it as quickly as you can."

"This looks wonderful," Armstrong announced, regarding the fish in front of him with unabashed delight. "Miguel has done a superb job."

He leaned into Tree, lowering his voice conspiratorially. "But don't ask him for the recipe."

18

"I don't know why I have to keep repeating this, but just to confirm what I've been telling you for years," Freddie said when Tree arrived back at Andy Rosse Lane much later that afternoon.

"Remind me," Tree said.

"You're batshit crazy."

"I don't remember the batshit part."

"Given the continuing situation involving your craziness, I've recently added batshit," Freddie said.

"I admit there is a certain amount of evidence in favor of that accusation," Tree admitted.

"I can't believe you took the case."

"I didn't have much choice. If I didn't take it, the Duckett brothers would find someone else. This way I can at least try to protect Scratch."

"You definitely need protection," Freddie said. "I'm not at all sure about Scratch."

Tree showed her the photos of Evka Bermann. Freddie raised her eyebrows. "She shouldn't be too hard to find, particularly if she's wearing that bathing suit—or hardly wearing that bathing suit."

"The trick is to find her with Scratch."

"I can easily understand why both brothers might want to marry Evka. But why would she run off with Scratch?"

"Scratch didn't say anything?"

"Nothing," Freddie said. "And when I was at the Blue Parrot, I wasn't in his room—"

Tree raised his eyebrows.

"I wasn't, Tree, for heaven's sake. Like I told you before, we met in the parking lot. There was certainly no sign of another woman. And while we're on the subject, I can't believe they paid Scratch three million dollars—even if she does look spectacular in a bathing suit."

"They weren't really going to pay it," Tree said. "But their goons messed up by grabbing me instead of Scratch. He managed to get away with the money—and Evka. My best hope is to find him, and convince him to give the Ducketts back their money."

"What about Evka?"

"My suspicion is they are more interested in the money."

Freddie gave the photos another look. "You think the Ducketts want their money back. I think you're wrong."

"Do you?"

"They want Evka. The men always want the woman they can't have."

"The wisdom according to Freddie Stayner."

"You think about your old girlfriends all the time," Freddie said.

"I do not," Tree protested. "Not since I met you, any-way."

"Liar." At least Freddie smiled when she said it.

Tree's cellphone began making sounds, saving him from further lame denials.

"What the hell were you doing with the Ducketts?" Scratch Callister did not sound happy.

"Where are you?" Tree demanded.

"It doesn't matter where I am," Scratch said angrily. "What matters is you're dealing with two very dangerous people you should not be dealing with."

"They want their three million dollars back," Tree said.

"Is that what they told you?"

"Along with Evka Bermann."

That stopped Scratch. There was a long silence on the other end of the line. "Listen to me, Tremain," he finally said. "With what I know, you don't want me as an enemy. And you sure as hell don't want to be involved with the Ducketts."

Tree felt his stomach tighten. "That sounds as though you're threatening me, Scratch."

"I'm trying to talk sense into you. Stay away from this shit."

"Shit you got me involved in," Tree retorted angrily.

"I didn't get you involved in anything."

"Tell me about Albert Aberfoyle."

"What?"

"Albert Aberfoyle. He's looking for you, along with the Ducketts."

"Well, I must say you've managed to get yourself into a shitstorm, old son," Scratch said in a calmer voice. "You have to get it through that rather thick skull of yours. Stay home. Love Freddie, and for God's sake, stay out of my affairs."

"Are you with Evka Bermann?"

"Stop asking silly questions I'm not going to answer." There was an edge to Scratch's voice. "I will tell you one last time—leave this alone. I know your secret, and you know mine. Mutual silence will only benefit both of us."

"We should talk," Tree said.

"We've talked enough, old son. Far too much in fact."

In the background, Tree could hear what sounded like an intercom voice: "Paging Mr. Patrick Diavolo. American Airlines paging Mr. Diavolo."

"I have to go," Scratch said.

"Scratch, where are you—"

But the line had gone dead. Tree looked over at Freddie. "You heard that."

"I heard most of it," she said. "What does he have on you, anyway?"

"He doesn't have anything 'on me,' as you put it."

"He seems to think he does—the secret he has kept all these years."

"He's delusional," Tree said.

"So, there's no secret?"

"I wouldn't call it a secret."

"Then what would you call it?"

"Something that's not as bad as he makes it out to be."

"But you won't tell me what it is," Freddie said.

"If I talk about it, it makes it seem more than it is."

"Okay."

Tree once again was saved by his cellphone from having to explain himself any more than he already had. He opened it up, thinking it was Scratch calling him back.

It wasn't.

"Tree, this is Detective Sergeant Cee Jay Boone." Her voice was cast in the familiar officious tone that Tree knew could only spell trouble.

"Sounds like they've given you a promotion, Cee Jay," Tree said. "Congratulations."

"I need you to come to the Blue Parrot Motel."

"At this time of night?"

"Right now," she snapped. "Get here."

Cee Jay hung up before he could object. Nobody, he lamented to himself, was letting him get a word in edgewise.

Freddie said, "I'd better come with you."

"I'm not sure that's a good idea."

"I do," Freddie replied. "With me there, they won't bring out the rubber hoses."

"Don't be too sure," Tree said.

19

The Blue Parrot Motel parking lot was filled with police emergency vehicles, a fire truck thrown into the mix for good measure should anyone mistake what was unfolding here for anything less than a major crime scene.

But what crime? Scratch? This is where he had stayed, after all. Tree's stomach tightened as he and Freddie got out of the Mercedes.

Ghostlike figures in white floated in and out of the glare of portable crime-scene lights that had been set up focused on the motel's façade and the open door to one of the rooms.

Cee Jay Boone appeared from somewhere in the surrounding darkness and approached Tree and Freddie. When Tree met her more than ten years ago, Cee Jay was a slim African-American woman with short-cropped black hair who didn't like him. A decade later she was a heavyset middle-aged woman with short-cropped black hair who sort of did and did not like him—depending on the circumstances. Tonight, circumstances appeared to require her not to like Tree.

Not a good sign.

"Tree, I'd like you to come with me," Cee Jay said peremptorily. "Freddie, if you wouldn't mind, I'd ask you to stay put."

"Sure," Freddie said.

"What's up?" asked Tree.

"Follow me," Cee Jay said, turning away and marching toward the motel. Tree followed through ranks of uniformed officers; the entire Sanibel police department appeared to have left their beds in order to be present, a sure sign to Tree that something big was afoot.

Cee Jay stopped at the threshold and indicated that Tree should go forward into the room. He stepped inside, squinting into more crime-scene lights that showed off Detective Owen Markfield in a white blaze of glory; the shining angel-descending image ruined by the angel's scowl—the one that, as usual, was aimed at Tree. Markfield had aged like everyone else during the past ten years, but he still managed to retain the blond good looks that made him camera-ready for a TV network crime series in which Markfield starred as the rock-jawed hero, albeit with a few more lines under his eyes and around his mouth.

Markfield didn't say anything. He merely pointed. Tree followed his finger to the spot between the double beds where the body lay in a pool of blood.

Albert Aberfoyle, his slim body adorned with the silver jewelry that had made him stand out at the Cattle Dock Bait Company, wore only boxer shorts and a pair of black socks. Tree made a note to himself that the jewelry would work fine, but otherwise he should never get shot to death wearing boxer shorts and black socks. Okay, maybe the shorts, but certainly not the socks.

He sensed rather than saw Cee Jay Boone behind him. "Well?"

"Well, what?"

"Tell me who we're looking at, Tree."

"His name is Albert Aberfoyle. What happened to him?"

"A smart detective like yourself might be able to see that Albert has ended up dead on the floor of the Blue Parrot Motel."

"Is that a bullet hole I see in his chest?"

"That would be a bullet hole, yes. Straight to the heart," Cee Jay said. "I have a question for you, Tree."

"You know me," Tree replied. "I'm always anxious to cooperate with local law enforcement."

"Why would the last call this gentleman made on his cellphone, why would that call have been to you?"

"I didn't get his call," Tree said.

"Why was he calling you?"

"He was a client."

Markfield couldn't resist making a dismissive sound. "Why would he hire you?" As if such a thing was impossible to imagine.

"He was looking for someone," Tree said.

"Who was he looking for?"

Who was Albert Aberfoyle looking for? Carl Chamuco? Or Samuel 'Scratch' Callister? Aloud, Tree said, "A man named Chamuco. Carl Chamuco."

"And did you find him?"

Tree shook his head. "Albert just hired me the other day."

"Let's get out of here," Cee Jay said.

Tree followed Cee Jay outside. Markfield nudged against him. If the rubber hose came out, Tree thought, it would be in Markfield's hand.

"The man in there." Markfield nodded back toward the room. "You say his name is Albert Aberfoyle?"

"That's right," Tree said.

"That's very funny, Callister," Markfield stated with a sneer.

"Why is that so funny?"

"We have him identified as Winston Dyab."

Tree gawked at the two detectives. "That's not what he told me."

"Well, that's who he is," Cee Jay explained. "We've been in touch with the New Orleans police. Dyab headed an investment firm that defrauded millions, mostly from Louisiana retirees. He'd been charged with fraud and was awaiting trial when he disappeared a month ago."

"Now he's here and dead," said Markfield. "And look whose name almost immediately turns up. None other than W. Tremain Callister, Sanibel's least-favorite, most-conniving, son-of-a-bitch private detective."

"Always good to know that I have the support of local law enforcement," Tree said.

"And this guy didn't say anything to you about who might want to kill him?" Cee Jay asked.

"He told me that his daughter's life had been ruined by the man he was looking for. He'd finally tracked him to Southwest Florida. He said he came to me because he wanted help from someone local who knew the area."

"Boy did he make a big mistake with you, Callister." Markfield had adopted his well-known sneering approach when it came to questioning Tree.

"Be that as it may," Tree went on, ignoring Markfield, "that's how I got involved with him."

Freddie came over to where Tree stood with the two detectives. She said, "It's late. If these officers don't need you for anything else, it's time we went home."

Neither detective looked happy. Freddie addressed Cee Jay. "What about it?"

Markfield's scowl only deepened, but Cee Jay shrugged and said, "Go home. We're finished here."

Tree started to turn away. Markfield grabbed his shoulder. "Don't tell me," Tree said before Markfield could start on him. "This isn't over."

"You bet your life it isn't, asshole. Something's not right here. You know how I know that?"

"No, Detective. How do you know?"

"You're involved. That's how I know."

———————

"You didn't tell them," Freddie said as she drove home.

"That the guy Albert Aberfoyle is looking for could be my half-brother? No, I didn't."

"The brother who may have murdered Albert Aberfoyle."

"Who, by the by, isn't actually Albert Aberfoyle."

"No? Who is he?"

"According to Cee Jay Boone, Albert's real name is Winston Dyab. He's wanted by the New Orleans police for defrauding retirees."

"Scratch could be involved—and that's why he killed Aberfoyle or whatever his name is."

"I'm not absolutely certain Scratch is the guy," Tree said.

"But you suspect he is."

"Scratch is many things, none of them very good," Tree said. "But I don't think he's a killer."

"He just steals three million dollars and runs away with someone else's wife."

"That doesn't mean he would kill someone."

"He wouldn't kill the man who tracked him across the country and might be getting in the way of three million dollars."

Tree didn't say anything.

"You think you know your brother—"

"Half-brother," Tree said.

"But do you really? I mean, Scratch turns up unexpectedly on Sanibel. He more or less tries to blackmail you to keep quiet about something that happened in your past. Then Albert Aberfoyle or whatever his name is shows up searching for someone who looks a lot like Scratch. You tell Scratch about him; he's furious. The next thing, Albert Aberfoyle is dead and Scratch is nowhere to be found."

"Like you said, he's got three million dollars and the wife of the Duckett brothers," Tree said.

"But if he runs, where does he go?" Freddie asked.

"That's what I intend to find out," Tree said.

20

The next morning Tree had to spend time talking Freddie into once again allowing him to borrow her Mercedes, convincing her that he would not damage the car, agreeing that he would soon get his own car. By the time he did all that and arrived at the office, Rex and Gladys were already in place—and looking pleased with themselves.

"It would be good if you came into the office from time to time," Rex said. "I'm supposed to be concentrating on becoming a world-famous bestseller, not running a detective agency."

"I was up late looking at dead people," Tree said.

Rex looked knowingly over at Gladys. "What did I tell you?"

"You said if there's a dead body on Sanibel, Tree's not far away," Gladys replied.

"My client," Tree said.

"That guy who was in here the other day?"

"Albert Aberfoyle. Only he's not Albert Aberfoyle, as it turns out."

Rex groaned. "Don't say anything else. I am too old. I can no longer deal with the complications in your life, particularly when they involve the dead."

"Let me tell you what I've found, Tree, thanks to Rex here." Gladys smiled fondly at Rex who looked uncharacteristically sheepish.

"I managed to get hold of a friend of mine at Southwest Florida International Airport," Gladys continued. "Based on what you told us about that announcement you overheard on the phone, we managed to establish that a passenger named Patrick Diavolo booked on American Airlines flight 496 to London, en route to Vienna."

"Vienna?" Tree couldn't keep the surprise out of his voice.

"That's in Austria," Gladys added knowledgably.

"Yes," Tree said. "But what's he doing going to Austria?"

"He apparently checked in with a woman—" Gladys paused to check her notes.

"Evka Bermann?" suggested Tree.

Gladys looked up. "That's not the name I got."

"What name?"

"According to my information, her name is Jana Teufel."

"When did they leave?"

"They caught a late flight to Heathrow," Gladys said. "There was a connecting flight to Vienna International Airport this morning."

That would have given Scratch enough time to kill Albert Aberfoyle, aka Winston Dyab, Tree thought, and then get on the flight out of Fort Myers to London.

That is if Scratch was a killer. Which Tree didn't think he was.

Did he?

As Tree pondered this, Jerry Delson, looking flustered, appeared in the office. "I'm on my way back to Sarasota," he announced. "I can manage things better from there." His gaze fell on Rex. "But not to worry, okay? We're going to hear the word 'no,' a couple of times before we hit the jackpot. 'No' goes with the territory. 'No' is the price of doing business."

"Who said no?" Rex asked.

"It's no big deal," Jerry said. "It's not a setback. These things happen. It's one moron at St. Martin's Press. A goddamn kid who doesn't know shit." He looked at Gladys. "Forgive my French."

Gladys said, "St. Martin's Press passed on Rex's book?"

"It's no big deal," Jerry said. "Young kid. Tells me no one knows who Joan Crawford is. I mean, come on. Who doesn't know Joan Crawford?"

"The book's not about Joan Crawford," Rex said quietly.

"They grab onto anything, these bastards. Bottom line, we don't want to be with them. They don't love the book. We want love. We move on."

"It's a goldmine," Tree said.

Nobody said anything.

"What do you mean you're going to Vienna?" Freddie said. It was dusk. They were seated on their terrace. Freddie was sipping her nightly glass of chardonnay. The setting sun cast her in gold, managing to make attractive the unhappy cast of her face.

"It looks like Scratch used the name Patrick Diavolo and flew there this morning."

"Let the police know," Freddie said. "They can get in touch with the authorities in Vienna and they can handle it from there."

"That's not what the Ducketts hired me to do."

Freddie looked at him in disbelief. "Are you kidding me? Tree, Scratch may have killed a man."

"As naïve as it may sound, I don't think Scratch is a killer. Maybe I can help him. To do that, I have to fly to Vienna."

"You're right, that does sound naïve," Freddie asserted. "You're forgetting that Scratch may be on the run and the last thing he wants is his brother showing up anywhere, let alone Vienna."

"Half-brother," Tree said. "And besides, there's something else just about as important."

"What else is there?"

"Evka Bermann."

"What about her?"

"The Ducketts want to know if they're together. He left town with a woman named Jana Teufel."

"And you believe Jana is actually Evka Bermann?"

"That's what I hope to find out."

"If they are together, what do you think the Ducketts are going to do about it?"

"For one thing, they will want their three million dollars back."

"And you think Scratch is just going to hand it over to you?"

"I don't know—I will know better once I'm in Vienna."

"If you're crazy enough to do this—"

"I don't think I've got much choice," Tree said.

"Tree, you *do* have a choice. But if this is the choice you've made—"

"I'm going," Tree said.

"In that case, I'm going with you," Freddie said.

"I don't think that's a good idea," Tree said.

"Too bad," Freddie replied. "I'm going."

21

The Vienna that Tree fantasized about, the Vienna at the turn of the century, what Graham Greene called "the old Vienna with its Strauss music and bogus easy charm," Klimt seducing the eager young women he painted, handsome army officers stealing away for an afternoon assignation at the legendary Hotel Sacher. That Vienna.

Or, even better, the post-war Vienna of—and here's Greene again—*The Third Man*, saturated with Anton Karas zither music and the haunted beauty of Valli. Although there remained hints of the turn-of-the-century Vienna—the vast Belvedere where Prince Ferdinand once roamed the vaulted halls before going off on that fateful visit to Sarajevo—Greene's Vienna in shimmering black and white, that Vienna had disappeared.

The Vienna of the 21st century, far away from Tree's fantasies, was a bustling modern European city that had no idea who Greene was—Strauss was stuck forever in the Viennese head—or what Tree Callister might be thinking in his romantic delirium.

"You're in fact too much of a romantic," Freddie pronounced, seeming to read his mind once they had checked into the Hotel Sacher and then retreated to an outside table at the Café Mozart to drink cappuccinos and watch the throngs of tourists.

"We're not here to be tourists," Freddie continued. "We here to find your, yes, I know, your *half*-brother."

"My failure in life is my insistence on seeing the world as a black-and-white movie with me moving through it in a trench coat, world-weary but incorruptible."

"Given the fact that despite your world view we are in modern Vienna, not knowing a soul," Freddie cautioned. "To that end, I did some research before we left and found someone I think will be able to help us navigate the city while we're here."

"What do you mean, you *found* someone?"

"A local private investigator. Emile Crabbin is his name."

"You're kidding," Tree said.

Freddie looked at her watch. "In fact, he should be here at any moment. I said we'd meet him at the Café Mozart."

"You hired a private detective? How much is he going to cost?"

"I'm investing in the Sanibel Sunset Detective Agency," Freddie said.

"I don't think you should do that," Tree said.

"Too late. It's already done. Are you angry?"

"I don't know what I am," Tree said. "Surprised, I suppose."

As though on cue, a short, rotund man in a rumpled blue suit approached. A neat black mustache was perched above a small mouth; the mustache along with the large eyes and a skull carefully covered over by strands of black hair gave him a somewhat cartoonish air.

"That's our man now," Freddie said, standing and waving. "Herr Crabbin," she called, "over here."

Crabbin smiled as he reached their table, offering his hand to Freddie. "Fredryka Stayner, Crabbin presumes."

Freddie nodded and indicated Tree. "This is my husband, Tree Callister."

Crabbin shook Tree's hand. "Herr Callister, your wife tells Crabbin you are a private investigator on this magical American island known as Sanibel."

"In a manner of speaking," Tree said.

"Crabbin was not aware of this Sanibel. However, thanks to the Internet, Crabbin has been able to investigate it thoroughly. It looks to be a wonderful place to live, a paradise, you might say?"

"It is that at times," Tree allowed.

"Not a place where Crabbin would immediately think there would be much work for an investigator such as yourself. Nonetheless, it seems there is enough to bring you to Vienna, a city where there is plenty of work."

"Is that so?" said Freddie. "Now why is that Mr. Crabbin?"

"Please, it is Emile." He gave her a knowing smile as he seated himself. "There are many secrets in Vienna and many people who would like to unearth those secrets, but do it as discreetly as possible. This is where Crabbin comes in."

A server approached and Crabbin ordered an Almdudler. "It's a carbonated drink made from elderberry," Crabbin explained. "Very popular. Although when off duty, a local beer called Ottakringer is a preference. They have been brewing it here since the 1830s."

He spoke to Tree. "Crabbin must tell you Herr Callister, he is most fascinated by the American private detective as portrayed in the literature of Herr Dashiell Hammett and Herr Raymond Chandler, Herr Ross Macdonald, and even Herr Mickey Spillane. These authors have been a great inspiration."

"And I don't know if you realize that your name Mr. Crabbin, is also the name of a character in *The Third Man*."

Crabbin's large eyes lit up. "Ah, yes, Crabbin is very much aware of that shared name. The movie is a great favorite. A masterpiece from Herr Graham Greene and, of course, its much-underrated director, Herr Carol Reed."

"I couldn't agree more," Tree said. "Shot right here in Vienna."

"Ah, but it is not the Vienna of Graham Greene any longer," Crabbin lamented. "Now it is the Vienna rebuilt after the war, the anonymous Vienna, the unrecognizable Vienna."

"My wife believes I am too much of a romantic," Tree said.

"The curse of us both, apparently," Crabbin said with a smile. "Crabbin finds himself lost somewhere in time, untethered in this city, floating, wondering about identity and purpose against this agonizing modernity."

"I'm hoping to visit some of the *Third Man* locations while I'm in Vienna," Tree said. "The Prater of course, and the sewers where the film's climax was shot."

"Crabbin would be only too pleased to show them to you, Herr Callister."

"Please, call me Tree."

"Then, a reminder, Herr Tree, to call me Emile."

"If I may be so rude as to interrupt this bonding of romantic reveries, we are here for the very real purpose of finding a man named Samuel 'Scratch' Callister," Freddie said, all brisk business.

"Ah, yes, many apologies." Crabbin looked embarrassed. The server arrived with his Almdudler. Crabbin ignored it and was abruptly all business himself. "Frau Freddie has previously emailed the particulars of the situation we are addressing today. Now after viewing your surname, Herr Tree, and the last name of this man Scratch, one cannot help but see that they are similar."

"They are indeed," Tree said.

"This is a relative of some sort you are seeking."

"My half-brother," Tree said.

Crabbin bobbed his cartoon head up and down. "And this Herr Samuel Callister, you believe he has recently arrived in Vienna using the name Patrick Diavolo, and he is accompanied by a woman named Evka Bermann. Is this correct?"

"It is," agreed Tree. "Although Evka may be using the name Jana Teufel."

Crabbin's head again made an up-and-down motion and his face took on a satisfied expression. "So, given Frau Bermann's surname, and the fact that this couple has come to Vienna, could her origins be in the city?"

"According to her former husbands, she is Czech," Tree said.

Crabbin appeared taken aback by this news. "Nonetheless, Crabbin took it upon himself to contact an old friend at the Vienna Police Directorate. He was kind enough to do a search to ascertain whether Frau Bermann has a criminal record of any kind."

"And does she?" asked Freddie.

"Based on a warrant issued by Interpol, the police here detained Evka, who was traveling under the name Jana Teufel, and a man named Winston Dyab. He was wanted in America by the FBI on charges stemming from a fraud investigation in New Orleans."

"Wait a minute," Tree interrupted. "You mean to say Evka was arrested with Winston Dyab?"

"She was using the name Jana Teufel, but yes, this is the information provided. This comes as a surprise?"

"It certainly does," Freddie said. "What happened to Evka?"

"There was no warrant for her under either name, thus she was released. Dyab, however, fought extradition to the United States. After being released from prison on bail, he disappeared."

Crabbin used the ensuing silence to sip at his Almdudler. He placed his glass on the table. "The two of you appear to be upset," he said.

"Surprised, is a better word," Freddie said.

"It could be helpful that the police provided the address Evka gave when she was arrested."

"It would be very helpful," Freddie said.

"Can we go around there?" Tree asked.

"Naturally," said Crabbin. "Although you should know the address is a year old. She may no longer be there."

"Let's find out," Tree said.

"When would you like to do this?"

"Now," Tree said decisively. "That is, if you're available."

"Of course. Crabbin is at your disposal. How can he not help an American colleague from a fabled Florida island who loves *The Third Man*?"

Tree waved for the bill. Crabbin finished his drink. "There is one other thing that has been a source of bother ever since Frau Freddie got in touch."

"What's that?" Freddie asked.

"The names you provided. Winston Dyab. Patrick Diavolo. Now Jana Teufel. Crabbin considers himself something of an amateur linguist. After Frau Freddie emailed the names, something about them struck Crabbin as strange."

"What about Jana?" Freddie was leaning forward, listening intently.

"In German, Teufel means devil. But it was Winston Dyab's name, the fact that he was from New Orleans."

"Yes?"

"Dyab is Creole for devil."

"And what about Patrick Diavolo?"

"Devil again, this time in Italian."

Freddie sat back looking somewhat stricken.

"Are you all right, Frau Freddie?" a concerned Crabbin asked.

"We should have seen that ourselves," Freddie said.

"Well, that is why you have retained Crabbin, to see the things you might not see yourself. That and to make sure you do not get lost in a city where, despite its patina of modernity, it remains in many ways as byzantine and mysterious as Herr Graham Greene and his *Third Man* found it in 1949."

"A city full of devils?"

Crabbin gave a gentle smile. "We have our devils, certainly. In mythology he is Krampus, the horned god of the witches. He survives to this day. We have local celebrations of him. Masked Krampuses have been known to cause, shall we say, disruptive behavior."

"Your friend with the police, he didn't provide you with a photograph of Evka by any chance?" Freddie said.

"In fact, yes, photographs of both the detained parties."

He fished an iPhone out of his pocket, fumbled with the screen for a couple of moments and then placed the phone on the table. The late Albert Aberfoyle struck a sullen expression for his mug shot. Jana Teufel wasn't wearing a bathing suit for her police photo. Nonetheless, it was easy to see that it was Evka Bermann staring somewhat alluringly into the camera.

22

Pötzleinsdorfer Strasse, lined with leafy trees, climbed a steep hill past an apartment block built in tiers into the slope. On the other side of the street was a park protected by a fence topped with barbed wire. What a barbed wire fence was doing in an upscale Viennese neighborhood was anyone's guess, Tree decided.

Emile Crabbin had no answer, intent behind the wheel of an Audi sedan that looked as though it had just rolled off the showroom floor and of which he seemed inordinately proud.

"Crabbin has always wanted one of these, ever since he was a child," he explained as he maneuvered the Audi against the curb just below the tiered apartment building. Prosperous neighborhoods were the same the world over, Tree mused. Like this one, they sat hushed and seemingly deserted.

Crabbin turned off the engine and with great satisfaction said, "The A4, is Audi's top-of-the line luxury automobile."

"The detective business in Vienna must be very good."

"Not that good." Crabbin blessed the statement with the ghost of a smile. "Crabbin was fortunate enough to inherit a little something from an otherwise distasteful aunt last year and decided to splurge a bit."

He pointed a plump finger at the tiered apartment building. "This is the address Evka Bermann gave to the police." Crabbin looked over at Tree. "Are you open to a suggestion as to what we should do next?"

"By all means," Tree said.

"Rather than the three of us barging in, allow Crabbin to visit the apartment and ascertain what the—how do you say?—the lay of the terrain?"

"Lay of the land," Tree corrected.

"Yes, that's it. The lay of the land. Ascertain what is the lay of the land."

Tree glanced at Freddie seated in the back. She looked at him noncommittally.

"This way," the detective said, "Crabbin is merely a local who has arrived at the wrong apartment, and we won't scare off your brother and Evka if they are inside."

The thought of confronting Scratch so soon after arriving in Vienna, dead tired from the flight, and with no plan what to do if he was in the apartment, made Crabbin's suggestion easy to accept. "Sure, that's fine, Emile. Just be careful."

"Crabbin is the most careful detective."

"You must have a talk with my husband," Freddie said ruefully.

As Crabbin opened the door, the loud music of a waltz emitted from him. Crabbin scrambled to get his cellphone out of his pocket and shut it down. "Apologies he said.

"'The Blue Danube.'"

"Ah," Crabbin brightened. "You know Strauss."

"I know the 'Blue Danube,'" Freddie said.

Out of the car, he adjusted his suit jacket and then trudged up the sidewalk to the staircase. He paused to glance back at Tree and Freddie and then started up the steps.

"I hope he knows what he's doing," Tree said.

"You're not mad at me for hiring him?" Freddie asked.

"No," Tree said, reaching back to squeeze her hand. "I should have thought of this myself. I wasn't thinking beyond getting over here and finding Scratch."

"Well, we're after him," Freddie asserted. "Supposing he's in that apartment, then what?"

Tree grimaced. He wasn't sure. Confront Scratch? Tell him he was in trouble and had to come home and face the music? And oh, by the way, hand over three million dollars. What were the chances of Scratch ever agreeing to that?

"Let's find him first," Tree said aloud. "Then we'll figure out the rest."

"Hmm," said Freddie, making the noise Tree knew too well: the I'm-not-convinced-it's-a-good-idea noise. "That's not much of a plan."

Tree was saved from having to respond by the return of Emile Crabbin, coming down the steps, hangdog expression in place.

He opened the door and slipped behind the wheel, issuing a loud sigh. "It is quite a hike up there."

"What happened?"

"Unfortunately, nothing," Crabbin said. "No one answers the door to Evka's apartment. Each apartment sits on its own terrace. Crabbin spoke to the neighbor below and he had no idea who was in the apartment above him, hadn't seen anyone coming or going."

"Well, we've gotten this far," Freddie said. "At least now we have an address which is more than we had an hour ago."

"That is much appreciated, Frau Freddie. Perhaps a suggestion?"

"Please," Freddie said.

"You have had a long flight, followed by our meeting, and then time at this apartment. Why don't you take an Uber back to your hotel? Crabbin will do what you hired him to do, remain here and watch the apartment. If either your brother or the woman accompanying him shows up Crabbin will call you."

Freddie glanced at Tree, who nodded. "But you'll call us as soon as anyone turns up?"

"Of course."

Ten minutes later, an Uber driver in a black Mercedes picked them up and drove them back to the Sacher. When they entered the lobby, the desk clerk motioned to them. "Herr Callister?" he inquired.

"Yes," Tree answered.

"There is someone waiting for you in the bar area."

"You're sure it's me?" Tree couldn't imagine who might be in the bar he might know or would know that he was in Vienna.

"You are Herr Callister?"

"Yes."

"Therefore, there is a party awaiting your arrival."

The sitting room adjacent to the bar was overhung with the sort of ornate chandeliers that could have dazzled the Habsburgs. A blond woman rising from one of the settees was caught in the pale light thrown off by crimson-shaded lamps.

Evka Bermann aka Jana Teufel said, "Mr. and Mrs. Callister. Welcome to Vienna. I've been waiting for you."

23

"This hotel is famous for its Sachertorte, but I must say I am not particularly fond of it," Evka said once they were all seated, Freddie with Evka on the settee, Tree facing them in one of the plush easy chairs.

"I'm sorry to hear that," Freddie said. "Tree and I were looking forward to trying it."

"I could be wrong, of course, you may find it absolutely delicious. Many people do. Presumably that's why it's famous."

"Well, it appears you're not fussy about the torte," Freddie said. "Perhaps you can tell us what you're doing here."

Evka flashed a smile, the winning smile, Tree suspected, that had brought both Duckett brothers to heel. "Why, I am here to see the two of you. Welcome you to Wien, as we locals call it."

"That's very kind of you, except we're not certain what to call you."

"No?" Confusion crossed that otherwise flawless face.

"Are you Evka Bermann? Or Jana Teufel? Or somebody else entirely?"

"Ah, perhaps I am the mystery woman, right? Is that how you see me?" She clapped her hands together to demonstrate her glee at the prospect.

"I see you as a woman with a lot of different names and motives to go along with them," Freddie said. "Pick one name and you're married to two rich husbands in Southwest Florida. Pick another and you're being arrested in Vienna along with your lover, Albert Aberfoyle. It's confusing."

The smile that won the Ducketts had disappeared. "I am known to my husbands as Evka, so I suppose that is who I am. As for Albert, I should tell you that was a misunderstanding—and he is not my lover."

"Do you know he's dead?"

"Yes, sadly." Evka looked appropriately downcast for a moment or two.

"Albert also had another name," Freddie went on. "Did you know him as Winston Dyab?"

"I was made aware of Albert's complicated past by the Viennese authorities," Evka said carefully. "That is when I ended my association with him." She threw up an elegant, dismissive hand. "You know, I believe I much preferred discussions of the Sachertorte."

Tree said, "Assuming we can call you Evka, how did you know we were here?"

"Perhaps a little bird told me." The coquettishness had returned. "Or maybe it was a phone call from silly Armstrong Duckett telling me he had hired a private detective to find me. I said, 'Armstrong, I can hardly be missing. I am on the phone talking to you.' He then demanded to know who I am with. I told him I am not with anybody." She made a tiny pout. "I am off men at the moment."

Tree said, "You're not with Scratch Callister?"

Her eyes popped with surprise. "Scratch? Who is Scratch?"

"You may know him better as Patrick Diavolo."

"I know Pat, certainly. But why would I be with him?"

"Because you are lovers?" Tree said.

Evka's smile wasn't so flashy this time. "You have been listening to my husband," she said with a sigh. "My estranged husband, I should say. The estranged husband who thinks every man who ever looks at me is my lover."

"He believes you are here with Scratch," Tree said.

"You keep referring to this 'Scratch.' I have no idea who you're talking about."

"My half-brother," Tree said. "Samuel Callister. Everyone calls him Scratch."

"Except you call him Patrick Diavolo," Freddie added.

"Whatever," Evka said with another dismissive wave of her hand. "I am afraid you are wasting your time here. My husband, my estranged husband, is angry and upset because I have left him. I'm sorry about that, but that is the way it is. I'm staying in Vienna. I'm not coming back to him."

"If I told you that that your husband paid Patrick Diavolo a lot of money to stay away from you, what would you say?"

"I would say that if my estranged husband told you that, he is lying."

"Then why would he hire me?" Tree asked.

"Because he is crazy," Evka said. She rose. Patrons seated in the corner beneath a painting of a sailing vessel navigating stormy waters didn't bother trying to keep their eyes off her. "He says he is in love with me, but he shouldn't be. I am not in love with him and that's the end of it." She blessed Freddie and Tree with one of her most winning smiles. "Enjoy your stay in Vienna. The city is not the city that it was once, but the Stephansdom is still there. You should make sure you visit before you leave." She started away, and then paused and turned. "And don't let me put you off the Sachertorte. Please try it."

And with that, she marched out, all eyes in the room following her.

———

As soon as they got to their room, Freddie jumped into the shower; Tree dozed. When she came out of the bathroom wrapped in a towel, Tree struggled awake. "What did you think of that?" Freddie asked, plopping herself down on the bed beside him.

"Of what?"

"Of the unexpected visit from the gorgeous Evka."

"I'm not sure what to think," Tree said.

"You think she is telling the truth about not being with Scratch?"

"Evka could be telling the truth, I suppose. What do you think?"

"I think you kept seeing her in a bathing suit."

"That's not true," Tree protested.

"I also think she's lying through her teeth," Freddie stated decisively. "She came here to throw us off the trail."

"What makes you think she's lying?"

"For starters, according to what your new assistant, Gladys, uncovered, Scratch left for Vienna with a woman named Jana Teufel. The same Jana Teufel who was detained by the Viennese authorities."

"That's not necessarily Evka Bermann in Vienna with Scratch," Tree said.

"Also, and this is most important, I just plain know she's lying."

"You think because she's beautiful and beautiful women can get away with lying."

"Particularly when they are lying to men," Freddie said. "Men like you."

"A happily married man like myself," Tree countered

"Who believed her," Freddie said.

"I'm not saying that, necessarily."

"Face it, my darling, you can still be dazzled by a pretty face."

"I am dazzled only by one pretty face."

"Liar," Freddie said.

"I'm too tired to argue," Tree said lying back on the bed.

The bedroom phone was like a banshee call that scared the hell out of him.

"Better answer it," Freddie said. "It could be our man Crabbin."

But it wasn't Crabbin. "Where are you?" Rex Baxter demanded.

"And hello to you, too," Tree said.

"Don't tell me where you are," Rex said.

"Okay," Tree said. "But you know where we are."

"No, I don't."

"Why don't you?"

"Because otherwise I'd have to lie to the cops."

"Why should you have to lie?"

"Because they want to know where you are. They were around to the office this afternoon with a search warrant. I suspect they've been at your house, too."

"What's going on?"

"The usual. The usual being you're in more shit. That's why I'm calling you from the Lee County Courthouse where they have the only pay phones left in Southwest Florida."

"Why are you calling me from a pay phone?"

"So the cops won't be able to trace this call, dummy. They're looking for you. Like I say, I don't know where you are."

"Why are they looking for me?"

"I'm just guessing here, but I think they've found something that links you to the murder of your client."

"Albert Aberfoyle?"

"How many murdered clients do you have?"

"Why would I kill Albert Aberfoyle?"

"I have no idea," Rex said. "But somehow the cops think you did."

"Shit," Tree said.

Beside him, Freddie tensed. "What's wrong?"

"The police are looking for me," Tree said. "Apparently, they now believe I killed Albert Aberfoyle."

"Why would you kill him?" Freddie asked in a voice choked with a combination of amazement and irritation.

Tree said into the phone, "What did you tell them, Rex?"

"I told them I hadn't seen you and I don't know where you are. Which I don't. Because you're not going to tell me."

"Thanks, Rex," Tree said.

"In the meantime, I've got Gladys with me. She has information she wants to share with you."

Gladys came on the line. "I've done some research into those names. I mean there's some weird shit going down, Tree."

"The devils," Tree said.

"You know? I mean, this is getting really scary if we're into devil stuff. That's like true evil."

"Gladys, there is no such thing as the devil," Tree said.

"That's what you say. But I've lived in Southern California, a place full of devils. Tell people out there that the devil doesn't exist, they would beg to differ with you."

"Look, I'm not sure where all this is leading, that's what we're all working to find out. But I highly doubt it involves the devil."

"Even if there's no devil, there are lots of really bad people who *think* they are the devil. And I hate to say it, Tree, but I have this awful vibe when it comes to your brother."

"He's not the devil, if that's what you're getting at."

"There's more," Gladys said. "This guy Lobo Salvador who is on the BlackHeart website."

"What about him?"

"They've got him listed as 'Watcher.' I wondered what that was all about. Watching what? Anyway, I did some digging."

"What did you find?"

"For what it's worth, Watchers were originally two hundred angels whose job it was to oversee events on earth. Anyway, they got corrupted by women, of course, couldn't keep their hands off them and were banished to caves where they will be judged at the end of time. Meanwhile, however, they occupy themselves spreading sin and corruption around the world."

"What are you getting at, Gladys?"

"Supposing that's what BlackHeart's doing, spreading sin and corruption, led by the Watcher himself, this guy Lobo? Confusion, confrontation, disruption, right?"

Tree thought back to the night he met Lobo. Was he spreading sin and corruption that night? Or lending a helping hand? Tree would have said the latter. "I don't know," he said aloud. "It all seems pretty farfetched."

"Maybe so," Gladys said. "But you know it's not always what's real that drives a guy like Lobo and maybe Scratch, too. It's what they convince themselves is real."

"Thanks for all this, Gladys."

"Just be careful. Okay?"

"I'm always careful," Tree said.

Gladys chuckled. "That's not what Rex says."

"What does he know?" Tree said.

"What was that all about?" Freddie asked after Tree hung up the phone.

"Gladys suspects Scratch is the devil."

"Well, it wouldn't be the first time that's been suggested."

"Come on, he's my—"

"I know he's your half-brother, but even so…"

"She also thinks the guy I met out in the Everglades, Lobo Salvador is an angel banished from heaven and left to sow sin and corruption around the world."

Freddie gave him a look. "That's too much, even for me." She stretched out on the bed. "Besides, I'm too tired for existential debates about the existence of evil."

"There is evil, as we both know," Tree said. "I simply doubt whether anyone called the devil has much to do with it. Or that angels transformed into the devil."

Freddie began snoring softly. Tree closed his eyes.

It was as if a light switch had been turned off.

24

In front of him on a moonless night was a dark, cobblestone street. Figures darted past casting long shadows while a whistling wind swept along old newspapers. Tree, shivering in the cold, huddled against the dark façade of an apartment building. Above him, someone threw open a window shining a stream of light, illuminating a man in a doorway. Tree could see that the man wore a black fedora and a long black coat. It took a moment to realize it was Scratch. Tree called out to him but as he crossed the street, the light from above was extinguished and the doorway fell dark.

Tree stopped, hearing footsteps running as he glimpsed a long shadow disappearing. Scratch escaping. He called out again, but the shadow just kept moving. Tree started after him, running full out to the end of the street.

Upright steel teeth surrounded an opening in the cobblestones. Tree could make out a descending iron staircase. He went down, following the winding staircase, his feet clanging against the metal steps. At the bottom, a walkway crossed a torrent of water gushing through a tunnel, vanishing into the gloom—and he suddenly knew where he was.

He had descended into the fabled sewers of Vienna.

Tree came off the walkway onto a ledge running above a shallow stream glinting in the light coming from further along the cavernous tunnel. A man suddenly lunged toward him, captured against the light. For a moment, he thought it must be Scratch, but as he drew closer, Tree saw that it wasn't Scratch.

Or it wasn't quite Scratch.

A cherubic face not unlike Scratch's was in shadow beneath the fedora, the gleam in his eye was similar to Scratch's, as was the smirk on his lips.

But it wasn't Scratch.

What Tree had thought was a black coat was in fact a long cape swept over the stranger's shoulders and falling as far as his ankles.

"I was beginning to think you were following me," the stranger said in a merry voice, again, not unlike Scratch's irritatingly merry voice.

"I thought you were someone else," said Tree, feeling curiously embarrassed.

"Well, am I someone else? I'm not so sure about that," said the stranger. "What were you thinking?"

"That you were my brother—my half-brother that is."

"A kindred spirit, old man," the stranger said. "He's very much at home down here, as am I. But then I've always been at home in these places. What about you? Are you like your brother, by chance?"

"No," Tree protested. "I'm nothing like him at all."

"Are you so sure about that?" asked the stranger. "You're down here, aren't you, with the rest of us?"

"It's an accident," Tree said. "I followed you because I mistook you for someone else. No more to it than that. I don't belong down here."

"Don't you?" His eyebrows arched beneath the fedora. "A case of mistaken identity lures you here? Or is it something else? You don't mindlessly follow someone into a sewer; you have to want to be here and when you want it, well, that's when you discover you can't get out again, and we have you."

"But you don't have me, and I can get out." Tree said in alarm. "It's an accident, I tell you. I didn't mean to come down here."

"But here you are, old man." That irksome Scratch-like smile played at the stranger's lips. "You might as well stay. You'll come down eventually, anyway. Trust me. Why fight it?"

"No," Tree cried. "I don't want to be here. I can walk away. I can—"

"No, you can't, old man. You are at the place where you've always been headed—a lifetime of descending into the depths of hell. Welcome!"

The stranger's cackling laughter echoed through the tunnel. Tree cried out—

"Tree," a familiar voice called. "Tree!"

Tree opened his eyes. Freddie hovered above him, her face etched with concern. "Tree, are you all right?" she asked.

"I was in hell," Tree said.

"You were having a bad dream," Freddie said.

"Or maybe it was the Vienna sewer," he said, sitting up. "You know, like the one in *The Third Man.*"

"It's as I've always suspected about you." Freddie straightened from the bed. "You've seen too many old movies."

"You can't see too many old movies," Tree said.

"In your case, I'm afraid you can," Freddie said.

"Initially, I thought it was the devil, but it may have been Orson Welles." Tree was sitting up in bed. "Or maybe it was the devil and he just looked like Welles—and a little bit like Scratch, too."

"Come on, rise and shine," Freddie said. "While you lingered in the sewers of Vienna, I've been getting hungry for some breakfast."

"Actually, when I think about it, Scratch looks a bit like Orson Welles. Don't you think?"

"Tree, get dressed," Freddie said.

Tree was no sooner out of bed than his cellphone issued unwelcome noises. "Herr Tree, it is Emile Crabbin calling, *guten morgen.*"

"Where are you, Mr. Crabbin?"

"Please, Emile. The Café Weinwurm near the main entrance to the Stephansdom. Is it possible for us to meet there?"

"We're just pulling ourselves together," Tree said.

"Why don't we say in an hour? Crabbin will keep one of his keen eyes out for you."

"We'll be there," Tree said.

After he hung up, Freddie looked at him questioningly. "The game's afoot," Tree announced.

"Thank you, Sherlock," Freddie said with a roll of her eyes.

"He does look like Welles," Tree said insistently.

"What?"

"Scratch. The more I think about it, the more I think he resembles Welles. Not the fat Welles I used to see hanging around Ma Maison in Los Angeles. The slimmer Welles from *The Third Man.*"

Another roll of her eyes expressed what Freddie was thinking.

25

"Crabbin remained in place until midnight," the detective explained once Freddie and Tree were seated with him at the café and had ordered coffee and croissants. The magnificence of the Stephansdom in bright morning light loomed behind them.

Crabbin tossed up his hands in resignation. "It is a very quiet neighborhood. Almost no one came or went at that apartment building. Certainly no one who matched the photos provided. If the man and woman you are seeking are there, they failed to make an appearance while Crabbin was present."

"In fact, Evka Bermann showed up at the hotel," Tree said.

Crabbin's eyebrows shot up in surprise. "Not what you were expecting, it is assumed."

"Not at all," Tree said.

"What did she tell you?"

"Not much," Tree said. "She denied that she was in Vienna with anyone, and insisted that a jealous estranged husband is lying."

"Well, that can't be true, can it?" Freddie cut in. "She never in so many words said she wasn't with Scratch. She just said we are wasting our time."

"Then Herr Scratch may be in the city, and this woman, this Evka, could simply be avoiding the truth, telling you something that would put you off your search for Herr Scratch."

"In America, we call it lying," Freddie said.

Crabbin's small eyes lit up. "Ah, just so," he said. The glow was extinguished a moment later. "The question this morning is this: what would you like to do now? Return to the apartment and continue what they call in American detective novels, the stakeout?"

Freddie and Tree traded glances. Tree's cellphone began to make noises. When he opened it up, a voice asked, "Mr. Collins?"

Tree groaned. "Callister. It's Tree Callister, Mr. Duckett."

"Call me Custer," Custer Duckett said. "And I apologize. I'll get your name right yet, that I can promise you."

"It might be easier if you call me Tree."

"Yes, yes it would at that. You mentioned that before, did you not?"

"I did."

"Well, Tree, I am calling to ask how you're doing over there."

"Possibly I would be doing better, Custer, if your brother hadn't told his wife that we're here looking for her."

"Ah, that means you have met with her. Is she with that monster?"

"She says I'm wasting my time in Vienna."

"She would say that, wouldn't she? My ex-wife is a duplicitous liar, Tree. You mustn't believe a word out of her mouth."

"Then you want me to pursue this?"

"Yes, of course I do. My brother is most angry at the thought of these two together, particularly given the amount of money paid to that bastard so that he would stay away from her. We are both counting on you to get results."

"I'm doing my best," Tree said. "A local detective I've hired has found an address where we think Evka is staying. We're staking it out, waiting to see if the man—"

"Your brother," interrupted Custer.

"My *half*-brother. In case my half-brother shows up."

"Make sure you get photographs when he does," Custer Duckett said.

"We're on the case this morning," Tree said.

"Good to hear. Make sure you call me as soon as you ascertain his whereabouts and whether or not Evka is with him."

"For the sake of argument," Tree said. "Supposing Scratch and Evka aren't together. Supposing Evka is with someone else."

"I doubt that will be the case. Just make sure you get photographs."

Custer hung up.

"Crabbin possesses a Praktica digital camera with a long lens that he has in his car," Crabbin said.

"I don't know about this," Freddie said. "Maybe Evka is right. Maybe the Ducketts are a pair of lovesick geezers and this is a waste of time."

Freddie looked at Crabbin; he shrugged and made more helpless hand gestures. "Hard to know what to say. Your man could be lying low in that apartment, not coming out. Your employer sounds certain that he is here."

"There's no use the three of us sitting in a car," Freddie said. "Why don't the two of you watch the place today, see what happens, and then we can decide on next steps."

"What are you going to do?" Tree asked.

Freddie smiled and said, "I'm doing something even more important than watching an apartment in a Vienna suburb."

"What's that?"

"I'm going shopping."

From somewhere on Crabbin's body came the sound of "The Blue Danube." He looked embarrassed. "Excuse me," he said, withdrawing his cellphone from his inside-coat pocket. He gave the screen a mournful glance, and hit something. The waltz ceased and Crabbin shoved the phone back into his pocket. "This must be dealt with," he said wearily. "Please finish your coffee. Crabbin will return with the car in a few minutes."

"Thanks, Emile," Freddie said.

Crabbin rose to his feet. "Many apologies for any inconvenience."

"It's fine. Don't worry about it."

Crabbin turned to leave and as he did, he farted.

Crabbin continued toward the Stephansdom as if nothing had happened. When he was gone, Freddie looked at Tree and said, "We have hired a farting detective."

26

A late-morning mist clung stubbornly to the treetops along Pötzleinsdorfer Strasse. A large woman with a small white dog emerged from the mist, slowing to peer suspiciously at the two men in the Audi parked at the curb of a street that, if anything, was quieter this morning than it had been yesterday. Crabbin, his camera nestled in his lap, munched on a packet of nuts, washing the nuts down with bottled water while Tree fought his usual stakeout battle with the gods of boredom who would make him drowsy and try to put him to sleep.

Crabbin farted. He looked embarrassed and shrugged. "Many apologies. Morning gas. *Blähungen,* as we say in German. Perhaps too much wiener schnitzel last night."

"Don't worry about it, Emile," Tree said.

Crabbin ate more nuts. And farted again.

As the woman allowed the dog to lead her on down the leafy street, Crabbin's phone again echoed with "The Blue Danube." Crabbin looked irritated as he studied the screen. "Many more apologies," he said lifting the phone to his ear.

Tree could hear an angry female voice coming from the phone. Crabbin, tense, but trying to maintain a level voice, responded in German. He listened some more. The other voice sounded angrier than ever. Crabbin spoke again his voice rising in similar anger. He was breathing heavily as he paused for a fusillade of German coming from the other end.

Finally, he threw down the phone in disgust. "*Scheiße!*"

He appeared to realize Tree was beside him, looking on in amazement. He abruptly looked very embarrassed.

"Is everything okay?" Tree asked.

Crabbin shrugged. "A domestic situation. A girlfriend who is angry because Crabbin refuses to marry her."

"And what's stopping you from marrying her?"

"Crabbin's wife," Crabbin answered.

"Yes, that might be an impediment," Tree agreed.

"Unfortunately, Crabbin's girlfriend is young and irrational and cannot see the reality of the situation. Or perhaps, more accurately, refuses to see that reality."

Crabbin leaned forward to retrieve his phone from the floor of the car. "What about you, Herr Tree?"

"What about me?"

"How do you handle the situations that arise with a girlfriend?"

"I handle the situation by not having a girlfriend," Tree said.

Crabbin put his phone away and looked at Tree in surprise. "You don't have a girlfriend?"

"Freddie has agreed to stand in for girlfriend duties, so another girlfriend is not necessary."

"This must be more of an American tradition than it is European."

"Either that or I'm happily married."

"So is Crabbin," the detective asserted. "Except of course for the complications of this present situation."

Crabbin farted loudly. He looked more embarrassed.

"*Blähungen*," Tree said.

"Indeed," Crabbin replied.

They sat in silence save for the sound of Crabbin's nut-eating. He finally finished the package, scrunched it up and carefully placed it in a bag he was using for refuse.

He brushed his hands together and sighed. "There is a way we might move this along," he said to Tree.

"What's that?"

"Let Crabbin go up the apartment and get inside. As soon as he has accomplished that, and the coast is, as you point out so helpfully, clear, he will call you. Together we can have a look around and hopefully you will be able to ascertain whether or not your man is in residence."

"How are you going to get inside, Emile?" Tree asked.

Crabbin gave him an impish smile. "Better you don't ask, Herr Tree. But a detective has his methods."

"Supposing someone is inside, then what?"

"Then Crabbin takes that risk and deals with it," Crabbin answered with a shrug. "But at least we will know. Besides, this person is hardly in a position to call the police. Is Crabbin correct about that?"

He had a point, Tree thought. He nodded and said, "Okay, Emile, but be very careful."

"Always careful, Herr Tree," he said unlatching his door. He got out of the car and then leaned in. "Crabbin will call you as soon as he's inside."

"Tell Crabbin I'll be waiting," Tree said.

The detective gave him a quizzical look and then trundled across the street. Through the windshield, Tree watched the detective, stooped slightly as though fighting the headwinds of life, reach the staircase and start up.

Tree checked his cellphone for messages. There were none. He held onto his phone, determined to keep his eyes open. Failing.

He was slipping away into sleep once again, when the phone sounded in his hand. "It is safe," Crabbin said in a whispery voice. "Come up."

Tree shook himself out of his sleep state and got out of the car. By now the mist had mostly lifted. He reached the staircase and began to ascend, the climb serving to remind him he was too old for this, making him wonder how Austrians of a certain age ever made it up these steps.

Winded, he arrived at the terrace where Crabbin waited in the doorway. "This way," he said and opened the door wider to admit Tree. Then he carefully closed it again and made sure it was locked.

Tree followed Crabbin along a hall, past a bedroom on the left, a narrow kitchen, and then into a sitting room, the light streaming through windows that looked beyond big green potted plants onto a lush garden.

Overstuffed crimson furniture crowded a room decorated with mounted plates, paintings, small stuffed birds. Shelves were jammed with books; every surface appeared to be covered with bric-a-brac of one sort or another.

Crabbin indicated that Tree should follow him back into the hall. A side table near the door was piled with mail and German magazines. Crabbin pointed to a sheet of paper, the printout of a boarding pass: Lufthansa flight 302 to London.

Tree was looking at it when he heard a noise from outside—a key turning in the lock to the entrance door.

27

Momentarily, Crabbin's face went blank, then he recovered and jabbed his finger in the direction of the sitting room.

As the door started to open, Tree followed Crabbin around into a second hallway that led off the sitting room. The two men pressed against the wall. A mirror on the far wall showed the entrance hall and reflected a young Asian woman, her waist-length hair tipped with blond streaks, dressed in black top and slacks, closing the door.

She paused, as though deciding what to do, and then advanced as far as the kitchen. She disappeared for moments and then was back in the hallway, going to the side table. Tree saw her pick up the boarding pass, fold it, and drop it into her shoulder bag. Then she started for the door and Tree began to slowly let out his breath until—

Crabbin farted.

It wasn't particularly loud, but in the mirror, Tree could see the young woman stiffen, and then come to a stop.

Tree held his breath again as she turned, her face a combination of concern and curiosity. She said something in German. When there was no response, she cocked her head, as though concentrating on listening.

Then she spoke in English. "Mr. Callister, are you there?"

Crabbin and Tree traded shocked looks.

Tree could see the woman advancing as she continued, "Mr. Callister, I know you are here. I saw the car out front. He sent me to get you."

Tree stepped sheepishly into the corridor. He sensed Crabbin behind him. "Who sent you?" Tree demanded.

"I'm not supposed to answer any questions. I'm only supposed to bring you to him."

Tree turned to Crabbin. "Only you, Mr. Callister. Not your noisy friend."

Crabbin whispered urgently into Tree's ear: "Herr Tree, please don't go anywhere without Crabbin."

"Mr. Callister will be safe with me," the young woman said. "I promise not to bite him."

Tree and Crabbin stepped into the hall. "It is not the biting that is concerning," Crabbin said with a frown. "It is perhaps the killing."

"I promise not to kill him, either." She looked at Tree. "Are you coming with me or not?"

"What's your name?"

"You can call me Lee."

"Is that your name?"

"Why not? One name is as good as another. We are wasting time. Please make up your mind."

"Do not go with this person, Herr Tree," Crabbin said in an anxious voice.

"It'll be all right, Emile," Tree said to Crabbin. "I will call you later."

"Yes, please. You must keep in touch."

Rather docilely, the two men followed the young woman named Lee out of the apartment, down the long flights of stairs and onto the street. She pointed to a yellow Jetta at the curb beside the park. "That's my car." Then she turned to Crabbin. "You aren't thinking of following us, are you Mr. Noisy?"

Crabbin looked at her and shrugged.

"I will take that as a no," Lee said.

"I'll stay in touch," Tree said to Crabbin.

Crabbin nodded and looked helpless as Lee went around and got in the driver's side while Tree slipped into the passenger seat.

In the car, she turned to him and said, "I must ask you this, Mr. Callister. Are you armed?"

"You would be amazed at how many people ask me that question," Tree said.

"You're an American," she said. "American men carry guns."

"I'm one of those unusual American men," Tree said. "I don't have a gun."

"I will take you at your word," Lee said.

She started the engine. The last Tree saw of Crabbin he was standing rather forlornly in the middle of Pötzleins-dorfer Strasse.

28

"Whose apartment was that?" Tree asked as Lee wound her way through a series of streets leading forever downhill.

"What?" she said with a smile, keeping her eyes fixed on the road. "You break into people's apartments without knowing who occupies them?"

"Do you know?"

She shrugged. "Somebody's mother by the look of the place."

"But whose mother?"

Another shrug. "Your guess is as good as mine."

Tree tried another tack. "Tell me how you're mixed up with Scratch."

"I don't know anyone named Scratch," she answered. "Therefore, I can't be mixed up with him, can I?"

"This is an interesting conversation," Tree said.

"Yeah. I'm a really interesting girl."

"Interesting enough to be involved with BlackHeart?"

When she didn't answer him, he said, "Is that a yes?"

"That's me concentrating on the road," Lee said. "The traffic in Vienna can be quite tricky."

"Like everything else," Tree said.

"They were right about you," she said.

"They? Who's they?"

"You really are way out of your league, aren't you?"

"I don't know," Tree said. "We'll see."

They rode in silence for the next twenty minutes until Lee swung the Jetta to a stop and Tree saw that he was at the entrance to the Prater, Vienna's best-known park. The iconic Ferris wheel, the Wiener Riesenrad, turned slowly against the bright blue of the noontime sky. "This is where you get off," Lee said.

"What now?"

"You walk toward the Ferris wheel."

"And?"

"And I suppose you get to demonstrate whether or not you are out of your depth," she said. "Get out, Mr. Callister."

"Will I ever see you again?"

"I hope not," she replied. "You're causing a lot of trouble."

"I've been accused of that a lot lately," Tree said.

"You should be a little more careful."

"I get told that all the time, too."

"Out you go," Lee said. "Before I say more of the things I'm not supposed to say."

"Thanks for the ride," he said.

Tree got out of the car and began walking. He proceeded along a wide avenue that in his mind at least led him from black-and-white movie memory into the modern reality of a commercial amusement park closer to Niagara Falls than it was to the bittersweet romanticism he always applied to *The Third Man*. What's more, the Wiener Riesenrad, the giant Ferris wheel where the luckless Holly Martins meets the suddenly very-much-alive Harry Lime, was now dwarfed by a much larger wheel that had no romanticism whatsoever attached to it.

There was a house of horrors featuring a bleeding skull and a green devil eagerly embracing a naked woman with a prominent derriere. The devil at play and enjoying himself immensely. The devil and his naked friend were the most egregious betrayal of an otherwise antiseptic Viennese sensibility designed not to scare off middle-class families.

Harry Lime would never recognize the place.

Tree reached the Wiener Riesenrad with its enclosed cabins rising elegantly above him, one of the few remaining nods to a long-gone Vienna—and for those to whom it might resonate, Orson Welles as Lime inside a semi-circle on the sign.

"Don't kid yourself, you're one of the few people who even remembers, let alone cares." Tree swung around to find Scratch Callister grinning insouciantly behind him, as though secure in the knowledge that he had successfully read his half-brother's mind.

A black suit had replaced his more casual Florida togs, and rather than the Borsalino hat a black fedora was tipped at a rakish angle so that it shaded his face and threw into doubt exactly what an onlooker might be seeing—precisely the effect, Tree suspected, Scratch had sought most of his life.

"That's all right," Tree said. "I still care. That's what counts."

"Well, you cling to that, don't you?" Scratch cast a hand in the direction of the Riesenrad. "Only the tourists ride on it these days, the older tourists at that. The local kids prefer the big wheel over there. Changing times, Tremain. Changing times."

"Except some things don't change, Scratch. They just get more confusing and complicated."

"You wouldn't be talking about me now, would you, bro?"

"What are you up to?"

"You know what I'd like to do, just to feed your nostalgia? I'd like to take a ride on the Riesenrad."

"I don't want to do that, Scratch," Tree said.

"Sure you do," Scratch insisted. "Tell you what, ride with me and I'll tell you everything you want to know—as well as a few things that probably never occurred to you and a few more things you probably don't want to know."

"What are you going to tell me, Scratch? Are you going to tell me you're the devil?"

"You already know that," Scratch said with a grin.

29

It wasn't busy and so they found themselves alone in one of the surprisingly spacious cabins, the machinery of the wheel grinding smoothly into gear, the structure beginning its upward climb, Vienna falling away, Scratch paying no attention, his eyes focused on Tree, perhaps trying to gauge his reaction to all this.

He said, "This is where I should mimic Harry Lime and say something about not being melodramatic, and point to the dots below us, asking if you would really feel pity if one of those dots stopped moving."

"Would you, Scratch?" Tree asked in all seriousness.

"What is it that Harry proposes?" Scratch continued. "I think in the movie it's something like twenty thousand pounds, a fortune in those days, for each of the dots that stopped moving. Today it would be, what? A couple of million dollars a dot? What about it, Tremain? If I said you could have two million dollars for each of those dots, would you really say no?"

"I'd say no, Scratch," Tree said, "but what about you? What would you say?"

"The age-old conundrum hasn't changed since Harry Lime was here," Scratch said. "Can you really bring morality into play when it comes to making lots of money? Harry had come to terms with the fact that the answer is no, you can't."

"Is that the conclusion you've reached?"

"What difference does it make, Tremain? You've already come to that conclusion for me, and I doubt I'm going to turn you away from it, although," he added with a grin, "I can certainly try."

"Does making lots of money include murder?"

That gave Scratch pause. His eyes narrowed. "What are you getting at?"

"Albert Aberfoyle is dead. Did you kill him?"

"Aberfoyle?" Scratch shook his head.

"Winston Dyab," Tree said helpfully.

"Good Lord, why would I kill that crook? Didn't I warn you not to get mixed up with him?"

"He was after you," Tree said. "He had tracked you across the country."

"And why would he do that?"

"You know why."

"Remind me, old son."

"He said you had destroyed his daughter, caused her to commit suicide."

"No one *causes* anyone to commit suicide," Scratch said disdainfully. "Certainly, I had nothing to do with what happened to that terrible woman."

"The police might think differently," Tree said.

"The police can think what they like." Scratch shot one of the smiles guaranteed to irritate Tree. "They might even suspect you, old son."

"Why would I kill Albert Aberfoyle?"

"Winston Dyab. Why, to protect me, of course. Your beloved brother."

"Half-brother," Tree said grimly.

"So you keep saying, old son. So you keep saying."

As Tree leaned against the railing running along the side of the cabin, Vienna was displayed in sunshine, his long-held movie fantasy meeting the reality of a glorious day unfolding outside the cabin, yet he was unable to take his eyes off his half-brother.

"What about the Duckett brothers?" Tree asked.

That drew a smirk from Scratch. "The Duckett brothers. Didn't I warn you to stay away from those two bastards? I guess you didn't listen to me, because here you are, doing their bidding—fool that you are."

"Nothing has changed since we last talked, Scratch. They paid you three million dollars to stay away from Evka Bermann yet here you are in Vienna with Evka Bermann."

"Simply because the fool Ducketts say I'm with Evka doesn't mean it's true."

"Are you with her?"

"I told you not to play the stooge for them, but here you are, hired to track me down and bring me to justice charged with what—moral turpitude? You really are a fool, Tremain. You wouldn't take two million dollars for each dot, yet you would work for the few bucks the Ducketts might throw your way."

"I wonder which of us is the fool, Scratch."

"Well, I'm the fellow with the three million, aren't I?"

"Like I say, Scratch, they want their money back. I'm here to get it for them."

"Let me suggest something, old son."

"What's that?"

"That you have allowed your jealousy of me, your fear, to be manipulated by these people. The Ducketts do no more than justify your worst suspicions about me."

"Like what, Scratch? Albert Aberfoyle believed you are the devil. The Duckett brothers aren't far away from the same theory."

That produced another smirk from Scratch. "Well, of course they're right, aren't they? At least as far as you're concerned."

"You still haven't told me what you're up to."

The wheel was on its descent now. Vienna, looking far too modern, drew closer. The dots were becoming human.

Scratch said, "What I'm up to is a business deal, and, yes, it involves Evka, and some people who wouldn't take kindly to your snooping around."

"BlackHeart? The Watchers? Are they involved in your so-called business deal?"

"The Watchers?" Scratch's smile was a little more forced this time. "You have been snooping around, haven't you, old son?"

"Are they?"

"Tell me, is Freddie with you?"

When Tree hesitated to answer, and perhaps place his wife in jeopardy, Scratch smiled knowingly. "Of course, she's with you. These days you'd be hesitant to go anywhere without her. You're in love with her, as well you should be. The question is…"

Scratch paused for effect. The cabin, Tree noticed, was coming in for a landing.

"Well, the question is, is Freddie in love with you?"

"Stop it, Scratch," Tree said.

"You know she came to see me at the Blue Parrot." Scratch's smile contained a hint of nostalgia. "It was a nice surprise, let me tell you."

"You bastard," Tree said.

"Nothing happened, of course. Freddie is far too loyal a soldier on the long march that is your marriage, but the sparks flew, I must say."

Tree swallowed hard, reminding himself that this was all bullshit, that this was Scratch knowing how to press his buttons, deftly able to get under his skin.

The cabin came to a smooth stop. The announcement was made in German and English. The ride on the Riesenrad was over.

"I'll give you this much," Tree said after taking a deep breath, "you know how to get to me, but then you always have known how to deflect attention from whatever crap you're involved in by trying to make me feel like shit. BlackHeart, Scratch. The Watchers. How are you involved with them?"

"Old son, I have no idea what you're talking about. What is this but a ride on a Ferris wheel, playing out a piece of movie nostalgia, you in the part of Holly Martins, naïve and unsure; me as Harry Lime, amoral, supremely confident. A nice contrast, don't you think?"

"Quit trying to talk around this."

Scratch blessed Tree with a smile. "I love Freddie, and you and I have a certain history together. So far, I've managed to keep you safe. But patience is wearing thin, particularly when you bring that goof Crabbin into the equation. Forget about BlackHeart and particularly forget about the Watchers."

"The fallen angels sent to corrupt humanity? Are you part of that?"

Scratch shook his head. "Get rid of Crabbin, pack your bags, check out of the Sacher, lovely hotel though it is, and go home. My further advice is to stay away from the Duckett brothers. Tell them you failed on your mission to Vienna. They're not getting their money back. Not that they will miss it. But be careful. If you're not, you may find them much more dangerous than you ever imagined."

"When I don't come back with their money—or Evka."

"She's not available and neither is the money. Sorry, old son."

The cabin doors opened. Scratch dashed out. Tree went after him, down steps and out into the amusement park where he was confronted by Lee, the afternoon breeze blowing her blond-tipped hair around her face. She pushed it to one side as she showed Tree the small pistol in her hand.

"Let well enough alone," she said quietly to Tree. "He doesn't want you following him."

"And to stop me you would shoot me?"

"I'm afraid I would," Lee said.

But Scratch was gone, anyway. Tree threw up his hands. "To hell with it," he said.

"I told you, you're out of your depth," Lee said.

Tree was beginning to think she might be right.

30

Tree stood alone outside the Riesenrad. Lee had disappeared along with her gun.

The sun blazed behind newly arrived clouds, drenching the park in a curious combination of light and darkness, as if a spell had been cast. Tree quickly dismissed that notion. No devils or spells here, just the all-too-human Scratch.

And the cellphone rescuing him from his own dark thoughts.

"Thank goodness," Freddie said when he swiped open his phone. "Are you all right?"

"I'm fine," he said. "Where are you?"

"Just outside the park," Freddie answered. "Where are you?"

"I'll come to you," he said.

He found Freddie waiting anxiously on the sidewalk near the entrance. She embraced him and held him tight with a mixture of relief and anger, the way she always did when she worried that he was dead and then discovered that he was alive.

"You said you were simply going to watch the apartment," she said.

"We were distracted by the usual things that distract me, a woman with a gun."

"And Scratch?"

"Scratch, too," Tree said.

"He's here?"

"Yes, I'm afraid so. Incidentally, how did you get here?"

"Crabbin, of course. He apparently was able to synchronize your phone with his so he knew your location. He contacted me, picked me up and drove me out here."

"Where is he now?"

"He dropped me and then drove off. He said to take a cab back to the hotel and he would be in touch." She gave him a searching look. "Are you all right?"

"I think so," Tree said. "Why? Don't I look all right?"

"You look like you've just had an encounter with Scratch," Freddie answered.

"He's a bastard," Tree said grimly.

"You didn't have to come all the way to Vienna to know that."

"He wonders if you really love me."

Freddie gave him a look. "Boy, he really does know how to get to you, doesn't he?"

"Not that I believe him or anything."

"You dope." She wrapped herself around him. "I love you. You know that. Whatever happens. Nothing changes that—not even the devil who shows up looking like your brother."

"Half-brother," Tree said.

———————

Returned to the Sacher, they retreated to the elegant blue confines of the Blue Bar, seating themselves on a plush blue settee beneath a gilt-framed painting of a woman who looked to Tree as though she had just polished off a slice of Sachertorte and had thoroughly enjoyed it. They ate potato chips from a silver tray. Freddie ordered wine; Tree ignored the waiter's frown when he asked for a Diet Coke.

"Coke Lite," the waiter sniffed before going off.

"Nobody in Vienna likes me," Tree said.

"You're feeling sorry for yourself," Freddie said. "I doubt the Viennese have thoughts about you one way or the other."

"I'm feeling fragile at the moment," Tree said. "I've just had to deal with Scratch."

Freddie put her hand in his. "Silly boy," she said.

The waiter returned with Freddie's wine and Tree's Coke Lite. They ate more chips.

"That will teach me to get on a Ferris wheel with Scratch."

"Were you Harry Lime or Holly Martins?"

"If you listen to Scratch, I'm Holly and he's Harry Lime."

"Yes, that sounds about right," Freddie said.

"I'm also the malevolent half-brother who is trying to destroy him because I'm jealous."

"I would not say you're jealous," Freddie ventured.

"No?"

"More like fearful."

"He's always scared me," Tree admitted. "Ever since we were kids."

"Why? I can see it now to a certain extent. But what happened when you were kids?"

Tree considered this for a time before he said, "Okay, the woman I thought was my aunt used to bring Scratch to Sanibel when my family vacationed there. It turned out she wasn't my aunt, she was my father's former wife, and Scratch was their son. Big revelation at the time—a shock, in fact."

"I'll bet."

"I wasn't sure what to make of it, and I was pretty upset, being only twelve at the time. There was a violent storm the night I found out, not a hurricane, I don't think, but pretty close. I ran out of the cottage we were all sharing. Scratch came after me. We were on the beach in the midst of the rain when it happened."

"What happened?"

"That's when the lightning struck."

"The legendary lightning strike."

"We were both knocked to the ground. Afterward, Scratch claimed he was actually hit by the lightning."

"Was he?"

"Put it this way, I allowed him to say he was. That's when it started."

"What started?"

"That somehow he was the devil's disciple—that's how his mother the healer felt about him."

"When she had him exorcised."

"I don't believe any of it, I really don't," Tree said. "What's more, I doubt he actually believes, but he uses it, and therefore he conducts his life accordingly."

"Is this the big secret that you've been keeping from me?"

"No," Tree said. "That's something else."

"That you still don't want to tell me."

"Not right this minute, no."

"All right, then," Freddie said. "I do believe more wine is called for." She summoned a waiter.

Crabbin appeared in the bar, his eyes lighting when he spotted Freddie and Tree. "Do you mind if Crabbin joins you?"

"Of course, Mr. Crabbin," Freddie said. "We've been waiting for you. Please, sit down. Can we get you a drink?"

"Yes, now that the day's work is done, a glass of champagne might do the trick."

The waiter arrived and Freddie ordered wine and champagne. The waiter nodded, happy in the knowledge that two of the three people sitting in his bar consumed alcohol. He cast what Tree was certain was a dirty look in his direction before leaving.

"The waiter doesn't like me," Tree explained to Crabbin."

"Alas, if you don't mind an observation, there appear to be a large number of people in Vienna who dislike you, Herr Tree." He gave Tree a reassuring smile. "Crabbin, of course, is not on that list."

"Good to know," Tree said. "What did you find out?"

"Crabbin did not listen to the instructions issued by that young woman you went off with. When this man Scratch emerged from the Prater, Crabbin was there and able to follow him."

"Where did he go?" asked Freddie.

"Straight to the airport. A Lufthansa Airways flight bound for London."

"He's headed back to Florida," Tree said.

"How do you know?" Freddie asked.

"I saw a boarding pass in the apartment on Pötzleinsdorfer Strasse."

"Was he alone?" Freddie asked Crabbin.

"It appeared so, yes. Our man went through security alone."

"But he could have met someone on the plane," Freddie said.

"That is certainly possible," agreed Crabbin. His champagne arrived in an elegant flute along with Freddie's wine.

Crabbin's eye relit as he lifted his glass. "*Prosit*," he announced. He took a deep swallow.

"Evka Bermann could have been on that plane," Freddie said.

"Yes, that is possible, certainly."

"Or she could still be in Vienna," Tree said.

"Also a possibility." Crabbin finished his champagne. "In any event, one thing appears to be the case and that is our quarry has departed Vienna."

"Why would he leave?" wondered Freddie.

"Maybe because we're here hunting him," Tree said.

Crabbin said, "The question becomes what will you do now?"

"Go home?" Freddie glanced at Tree for confirmation. "Scratch has left town, what's the point?"

"We go home without accomplishing much," Tree said, trying to keep the disappointment out of his voice.

Crabbin looked at his watch. "The hour is late. Best to be getting on. Frau Crabbin will be preparing dinner."

"Frau Crabbin?" Tree raised his eyebrows.

"Alas, Crabbin has no further complications that would interfere with his being a good husband. Therefore, Crabbin is headed home."

Crabbin stood. "Please call in the morning with news on what you've decided."

"Thank you for everything today," Tree said.

"Crabbin is afraid he was not at his best. Again, many apologies."

"It more or less worked out," Tree said. "Thanks to you, we at least know Scratch has left Vienna. We're not stumbling around thinking he's still here."

"Tomorrow, then," Crabbin said.

As he started away, Crabbin farted. He turned sheepishly to Tree and Freddie and gave one of his helpless post-fart shrugs.

"*Blähungen,*" he said.

And off he went.

"What was that all about?" Freddie asked when Crabbin was gone.

"Gassy. Too much wiener schnitzel, says Crabbin."

"No, I mean the stuff about going home to be a good husband again."

"Oh, that," Tree said. "His girlfriend can't understand why he won't marry her."

"Because he's already married?"

"She didn't seem to want to take that into consideration," Tree said. "I think they've now broken up."

"Maybe she didn't like the fact that he farts all the time," Freddie said.

"He was pretty upset," Tree said. "He wanted to know how I handled my girlfriends in America."

"What did you tell him?"

"I told him I handled my girlfriend by being married to her."

"Good answer," Freddie said.

When she finished her wine, she said, "If this is our last night in Vienna…"

"Yes?"

"We should at least have a walk around a bit, get some sense of the city."

"I was hoping you were going to suggest something else."

She grinned. "We can do that too, but first, a little sightseeing."

31

They wandered through the Stephansdom Quarter at sundown, the light hitting the four-hundred-and-fifty-foot gothic spire so that it blazed brightly as though touched by the glory of God. The crowd swirling around the shops and cafés on the streets around the Stephansdom appeared oblivious to any glories that might be striking their cathedral. Of course, reflected Tree, they weren't having to deal with a half-brother who could be the devil.

The crowds thickened along Kohlmarkt, everyone so young, Tree thought, filling the restaurants on either side of a thoroughfare dedicated, as were so many of the world's city centers, to the Guccis, Chanels, and Pradas. Hard to believe these kids could afford anything offered by the nearby merchants of haute couture.

"You're a long way away," Freddie said. "What are you thinking?"

"Simply marveling at how young the world is outside our little Sanibel Island bubble. How old I'm becoming. How out of it I am."

"Want to know what I'm thinking?"

"That I am still a sexy guy and I shouldn't worry too much about age because you still find me so hot?"

"In addition to that," Freddie said.

"Okay, what are you thinking?"

"I'm thinking about Evka Bermann."

Tree gave a surprised look. "What are you thinking?"

"More like I'm wondering if she actually got on that plane with Scratch."

"What would make you think she didn't?"

"Think about it. Your estranged husband has sent a detective thousands of miles to find you. She makes it clear she doesn't want anything to do with you. Then she turns around and flies back to the place where her husband is? I have trouble with that."

"Except she could be flying back because she is now with Scratch," Tree offered.

"I'm still having trouble."

"What are you suggesting?"

Freddie shrugged. "It's not that late. Why don't we revisit that apartment on Pötzleinsdorfer Strasse?"

"You think she's there?"

"If she is, you'd like to talk to her would you not?"

"Would I?"

"You would." Freddie held his arm tighter.

———

The Uber driver dropped them down the hill from the apartment building. Pötzleinsdorfer Strasse was a quietly haunted street at this time of night, intermittently illuminated in yellowish lamplight.

Tree and Freddie walked up to the apartment and stood looking at the wide staircase in pools of light rising into darkness. Freddie was having second thoughts.

"Maybe we are crazy to be doing this," she said.

"It would only be crazy if I had suggested it," Tree said.

"She's probably not even here. She's probably on that flight to London, nestled beside Scratch."

"We're here now," Tree said. "We might as well take a look."

Halfway up the stairs, Freddie paused at one of the landings to get her breath back. "How does someone do this every day?"

"Believe me, I've wondered the same thing," Tree said.

They reached the apartment. Freddie looked at Tree. "Well?"

He saw that the door was ajar. "Shit," he said.

"What's wrong?"

"The door. It's open."

Tree pushed the door wider, calling out, "Hello?"

There was no answer. Tree felt his stomach drop.

"What do you want to do?" Freddie, in a whisper.

An overhead light lit the familiar hallway. Beyond, the apartment was in darkness. Tree called out again. There was no answer. Freddie had her hand on his back as he moved forward. She whispered, "Tree, maybe we shouldn't do this."

But he kept moving into the plush red living room. The garden outside the windows lay in darkness. The only light came from the hallway. The body sprawled at odd angles in the big red armchair was naked, on display in shadow, drenched in blood.

The young Asian woman who said her name was Lee stared sightlessly at Tree. Her throat had been slashed.

Freddie gasped and her hand shot to her mouth to stifle that gasp. Tree said, "Let's back out of here. Do you have that cloth that clean surfaces?"

"If you mean the Norwex cloth, of course."

"Use it to clean the door latch on our way out."

"We're not going to just leave her here."

"For now, let's get out."

They backed out of the apartment. Freddie used the cloth to wipe the latch. They went down onto the street.

"Tree, we have to call the police." Freddie spoke in a tense voice.

"I'm calling Crabbin." Tree had his cellphone out.

"Crabbin? Why are you calling him?"

"Because we're strangers in Vienna with a dead body. We don't speak the language, and we're going to need someone who can run interference with the Austrian authorities."

Tree poked out the number and got Crabbin's voice-mail. "Emile, we're at Pötzleinsdorfer Strasse. There's a problem. Call me as soon as you can."

"Tree, we can't just leave that woman up there," Freddie said.

"Her name is Lee, at least that's what she told me. She's the woman who found Crabbin and me in the apartment. She drove me out to the Prater to meet Scratch. She pulled the gun on me when I tried to follow him once we got off the Ferris wheel."

"Tree, we're standing in the middle of a street. We have no idea where we are. There's a dead woman in an apartment. We've got no way out of here. Call the police."

Almost as soon as the words were out of Freddie's mouth, the discordant honk of a police klaxon disturbed the night. A pair of police cruisers, POLIZEI slashed across their sides, came screaming up the hill, moving so fast Tree thought for sure the vehicles would run over the two of them.

However, they managed to screech to a halt a couple of yards short of disaster. There wasn't a whole lot of time to be relieved as a third police car sped up the hill.

Then there were polizei everywhere, guns drawn, screaming orders in German. Freddie called out in the only German she could summon: "*Ich spreche nicht!*"

Tree and Freddie had their hands high in the air as more police cars arrived. Slowly, officers moved in, keeping their guns trained on the dangerous suspects. The officers forced them to the ground so that they could be handcuffed.

Tree tried to think of something to say, but all that came to mind were lines spouted by various Gestapo officers in the Second World War movies he devoured as a kid. The police in turn kept stating the one line he could translate from those movies: "*Schnell! Schnell!*"

Tree caught a glimpse of the desperate look on Freddie's face in the red and blue glow of police lights before he was pushed into the back of a Volkswagen Passat, a pretty small vehicle in which to contain a notorious criminal such as himself, he thought. He must remember to tell the Viennese police that he preferred to be arrested by American police if only because they had bigger, more comfortable cars.

Then he saw the hard expressions on the faces of the arresting officers and thought better of it.

They probably would not be interested in his views on police cars.

32

If anyone back on Sanibel was ever interested in the locations of police stations in Vienna, Tree felt confident to report that the nearest location was about ten minutes away from where he was arrested on Pötzleinsdorfer Strasse.

The headquarters from what he could see—and he only got a brief glimpse before the car in which he was a passenger dropped down a narrow passage into the depths of an underground parking garage—was in an imposing block on a street of imposing blocks. He had ridden in silence, having learned long ago and through painful experience that no matter which country you were arrested in, it was just as well to keep your mouth shut.

The realization that this was actually one of the painful lessons he had learned said as much as anything about the sorry turn his previously law-abiding existence had taken. What infuriated him even more was the thought that Scratch was on his way back to America, probably flying first class, eating good food and drinking fine wine while he languished in a smelly, anonymous interrogation room, his hands bound behind him.

As was usually the case, he was made to sit by himself for an hour or so, the police thinking being that the suspect—him—would stew in his own juices for a while, realize what kind of shit he had gotten himself into, and therefore would be much more cooperative when his interrogators appeared.

Sure enough, after little more than an hour, a short, slim man wearing glasses, dressed in a nicely tailored dark-blue suit briskly entered the room. He carried a file which he laid on the table in front of Tree before seating himself across from him.

"You say you are W. Tremain Callister." The man spoke in English. "Is this correct?"

"I am Tremain Callister," Tree said. "Who are you?"

"I am federal police inspector Fritz Gerhardt," he said, adjusting his glasses for emphasis. "I am in charge of the murder investigation."

"There's been a terrible mistake, Inspector. My wife and I should never have been arrested—"

"Let's get a couple of things settled so we can ascertain the facts and discover if there has been a mistake. To repeat, you say your name is W. Tremain Callister?"

"Why is that a problem?"

"Because Herr Callister, we have information that suggests you are not Tremain Callister but in fact Samuel Callister, better known to Interpol as Carl Chamuco or Patrick Diavolo."

Tree gawked in amazement. "You're kidding. You think I'm Samuel Callister?"

"Aka Carl Chamuco, aka Patrick Diavolo," Inspector Gerhardt said.

"That's my brother—my half-brother. This is a terrible case of mistaken identity."

"Is it?"

"Yes, it is. Check with my wife. I'm sure you have her in another interrogation room. If she hasn't already vouched for who I am, she'll certainly be glad to do it. Tremain Callister. Everyone calls me Tree."

That elicited a thin smile from the inspector. "Tree? Interesting. Well, Tree, we have spoken at length to your wife. She's been very cooperative with us."

"Good. Glad to hear it."

"She has confirmed that you are in fact Samuel Callister, aka Carl Chamuco, aka Patrick Diavolo."

"That's crazy," Tree said, noting that his voice was breaking and that he was having trouble catching his breath—sure signs of the stress he was feeling. "She would never have said that. You're lying, Inspector."

"She's also been helpful in laying out the details of what happened at Pötzleinsdorfer Strasse this evening."

"As she must have told you, we went to the apartment, found the door open, and when we entered, we discovered the body of the young woman. We were just about to call the police when the police arrived."

"That's not quite how she tells the story."

"What are you talking about? That's what happened."

"According to her, the two of you arrived together at the apartment. You insisted that she wait on the street while you went up to talk to the young woman, Kim Rada, your girlfriend from what we can ascertain."

"*What?*"

"Your wife, after waiting for some time, went up to the apartment, discovered the door open and went inside where she found you with the murdered woman. She was trying to convince you to call the police—something you were understandably unwilling to do—when officers arrived on the scene."

"None of this is true, it's crazy. She couldn't possibly have told you any of that."

"That is her story, Herr Callister. We have little reason to doubt her."

"This is all a put-up job to get me to admit to something that never happened," Tree insisted, trying to keep a level tone in his voice.

Inspector Gerhardt gave him a puzzled look. "I'm not quite sure what you mean by a 'put-up job,' Herr Callister. I am merely telling you what your wife has told us."

"Let me see her, let me speak to my wife," Tree said.

"That will not be helpful to either of you right now."

"You're afraid to bring her in here because what you're saying is bullshit. None of it is true."

Inspector Gerhardt gave him a long look before closing the file in front of him and rising to his feet. "Stand up, Herr Callister."

Tree rose and Gerhardt took him by the arm and led him to the door and opened it. "Come along, please," he said.

They went along an anonymous hallway to another door. Gerhardt knocked. A moment later, a young detective opened it and nodded at Gerhardt. "*Ja, mein Herr?*"

"Step inside, Herr Callister," Gerhardt ordered.

The young detective moved out of the way so Tree could enter the interrogation room. A woman sat behind a metal table. She looked up when Tree appeared and smiled.

"Darling," Evka Bermann said.

33

"This woman is not my wife," Tree Callister said.

"Darling," Evka Bermann purred. "I'm so sorry. I had no choice."

Tree glared in astonishment, his mind swirling. He turned to Gerhardt. "What have you done with my wife?"

"We have brought you to your wife, just as you demanded," Gerhardt said. "First you tell us you are not who we know very well you are. Then you tell us the woman who is your wife can vouch for you. When it becomes apparent that she can't, you then deny she is your wife. Do you really take us for such fools, Herr Callister?"

"This is not the woman you arrested earlier tonight. This is a woman named Evka Bermann. She is with my half-brother, Samuel Callister. I am not Samuel Callister. Or Carl Chamuco. Or Patrick Diavolo. Like I keep telling you, I'm Tree Callister."

Nobody spoke. Evka Bermann looked at the inspector and gave a helpless shrug. Poor, demented Samuel, that shrug seemed to say.

"All right, that's enough," Gerhardt announced. He took Tree by the arm and pulled him away. The door closed on the knowing face of Evka Bermann.

"Let's resume our conversation," Gerhardt said.

"This is so crazy," Tree repeated. "Crazy, crazy."

Gerhardt led him back into the interrogation room. He closed the door. Tree felt numb, the walls closing in on him.

Gerhardt left the room, leaving him alone. He stared at the white wall, the searing whiteness of the wall. Okay, he thought, forcing himself to clear away his growing sense of panic. Think straight, he told himself. Something has happened, something that he could not help thinking involved Scratch's conniving. But what? And where was Freddie? What had they done with her?

Then Gerhardt was back. He leaned against the wall, folding his arms, contemplating Tree as though studying a fascinating example of one of those very bad persons found only in America.

"You are perhaps aware, Herr Callister, that Austria has one of the world's lowest murder rates," the inspector said. "Murder is something quite rare here. No one kills anyone in this country."

"I wasn't aware of that," Tree said.

"Now you, an American, from a place where everyone kills everyone else, you come to my country, to my city, and no sooner do you arrive than you murder one of my citizens." He unfolded his arms as he spoke, his face darkening. "This, Herr Callister, is unacceptable. Do you understand? *Totally* unacceptable."

"I didn't kill anyone," Tree said slowly. "As I have told you, my wife and I found the body when we went to that apartment. The woman in the other room is Evka Bermann, also known as Jana Teufel. The Viennese police held her for Interpol under that name several years ago. She is not my wife. But you must know that. You're lying to me about all this. I'm not quite sure why, but you are lying. Either that or someone has managed to cleverly pull the wool over your eyes."

Gerhardt looked bewildered. "What is this pulling wool?"

"Fooled you. Made one believe something that isn't true—trying to make *me* believe what isn't true."

Gerhardt responded with a resigned sigh and a shake of his head. Without another word, he left the room.

Time passed. Tree wasn't sure how long. The handcuffs chafed his wrists, his muscles ached. He tried to think through his predicament, employing logic, immediately realizing logic wouldn't work. There was no logic to any of this.

He shifted around in his seat. His arms ached even more, and now his legs were in pain, too.

Then the lights went out in the room. "Hey," he called out. "Turn on the lights. Okay?"

No one answered. He remained in darkness. He wanted to shout some more, but shout what? *Where is everybody? Let me out of here?*

Free Tree Callister?

Yes, that was it. That would do the trick.

"*Free Tree Callister!*" he shouted. And then he added: "*You bastards!*"

It didn't do any good. No one answered. The silence roared back.

Eventually, he did what he had an uncanny knack for doing in even the most dangerous situations once boredom set in—he dozed off.

How long he was out, he wasn't sure. The sound of the door opening jerked him awake. He blinked into the shaft of light coming from the corridor. The figure of a uniformed officer darkened the doorway. He said something in German and then stepped inside and Tree saw that he was holding a key. He used it to unlock Tree's wrists. As soon as the handcuffs fell away the relief was instant, but short-lived.

The officers unceremoniously jerked him to his feet. "*Bewegen sie bastard.*"

When Tree didn't move fast enough, uncertain what was happening, the officer gave him a hard shove into the corridor. They went along to a door. The police officer pushed Tree against the wall and then pressed a series of numbers on a key pad. There was a clicking sound and then the door popped open. The officer indicated for Tree to go through. "*Verpiss dich hier,*" he said.

"What is this?" Tree demanded. "What's going on?"

In response, the officer gave him another shove, out the door this time. Tree found himself on a stoop overlooking an alleyway. It was nighttime. The door slammed behind him.

Tree moved down the steps. It was very dark but not so dark Tree couldn't see the outline of an Audi sedan and the man leaning against the hood, lighting a cigarette.

The flare of the match against the end of the cigarette was enough to briefly illuminate Scratch's face. Tree could only stare in disbelief. Scratch smiled and said, "Surprise, old son."

"You bastard," Tree said.

"That's actually probably true," Scratch said. "I don't believe our father ever married my crazy mother. But that's another story."

"What the hell is all this about? And where's Freddie?"

"Freddie is fine. Freddie is safe. No thanks to me. And comes to that, you can thank me for once again saving your ass."

"Don't give me that," Tree said angrily. "You got me into the shit in there. Whatever it was supposed to be."

"It was supposed to be powerful men taking care of me," Scratch said. "Luckily, they got their wires crossed."

"With some help from your friend, Evka."

"Unfortunately, as has been the case with most of the women in my life, Evka has turned out to be untrustworthy. Luckily for the two of us, I know enough people who know the right people who were able to straighten things out. Unfortunately, your inability to keep your nose out of this has resulted in me having to delay my exit from Vienna, not good at all, I have to tell you."

"Why? Because you killed Kim?"

Scratch gave him a disdainful look. "Please. As you have already seen, certain people would have liked to make it seem as though I killed her. And I would have been at her apartment had I not been on the way to the airport."

"I thought you were on a plane."

"As I stated, I've put myself in jeopardy thanks to the phone call that forced me back to once again come to your rescue."

"I didn't need rescuing. No matter what stupidity was cooked up, the fact is I'm not you, and eventually they would have realized that."

"Eventually could have been a long time." Scratch gave a sigh "But have it your way. I must get out of here."

"Where are you going?"

"No concern of yours, old son." He pointed to the Audi. "Get in."

"I'm not getting into any car until I know about Freddie."

"The car will take you to Freddie. Get in before the people in there change their minds."

Scratch started away, casting a long shadow across the brick wall, the star of his own noir mystery, Tree thought. He called out. "What about the Watcher?"

Scratch paused as though deciding what to say.

"What about it, Scratch? Are you the Watcher?"

"No, I'm not. But a word of advice: I'd be very careful around anyone who is."

The engine came to life and its headlights flared. Caught in the bright light, Scratch started away.

Tree called again: "What happens if I'm not careful?"

"Then the Watcher watches, the devil pays, and Tremain Callister dies."

And he was gone.

A voice behind him said, "This way, Herr Tree."

Tree swung around and through the glow from the headlights, he could see Emile Crabbin motioning to him from the open driver's-side door.

"Time to go," Crabbin said.

"What the hell," Tree said. "What are you doing here?"

"We must hurry, Herr Tree. Otherwise, you will miss your flight. Frau Freddie is waiting at the airport."

Tree hesitated, his mind swirling with confusion.

"Come, please," Crabbin called anxiously. "There is not much time!"

"Tell me how you figure in tonight's madness," Tree demanded as Crabbin drove through deserted Vienna streets.

"Best to say that Herr Diavolo, as he insisted on being called, enlisted Crabbin's aid to help him facilitate matters after you had been arrested in connection with the murdered woman at Pötzleinsdorfer Strasse."

"You're working for him," Tree pronounced.

"Working for *you*, Herr Tree. When it became apparent Herr Diavolo wanted to help, then Crabbin cooperated with him. Certain important people at the federal police were persuaded to release Frau Freddie. Arrangements were quickly made for a flight out of Vienna. Frau Freddie returned to the Sacher, packed your bags and checked out.

Crabbin then drove her to the airport. At that point, Herr Diavolo was in touch with instructions to meet him at police headquarters."

"And now here you are," Tree said.

"It has been a most curious night," Crabbin said.

"You must wonder what's going on," Tree said.

"Crabbin does not wonder. Crabbin serves his client, whatever that client's curious needs might be."

"And my needs at the moment?"

"To get you out of Austria as soon as possible."

"Doesn't look as though I have much choice," Tree said.

"No choice at all, Herr Tree," Crabbin said.

When they arrived at the Vienna Airport's departures level, Crabbin said, "Frau Freddie awaits at the British Airways counter. She has your passport and your ticket. Good luck, Herr Tree."

"Thank you, Emile," Tree said. "You've been a great help."

Crabbin shrugged. "Crabbin is not so sure about that, but your thanks are appreciated. You are probably no wiser now than you were when you arrived, but at least you are alive."

"So far," Tree said.

He got out of the car and as he did, Crabbin leaned over and said, "Herr Tree, one final observation if you don't mind."

"What is it, Emile?"

"Krampus," Crabbin said.

"The devil."

The detective nodded. "Crabbin hopes that in leaving Vienna you are flying away from danger, but if Herr Diavolo is anywhere nearby, then you are almost certainly flying into it."

"Let's hope not," Tree said.

"Please, be very careful as you proceed, Herr Tree."

"Everyone wants me to be careful," Tree observed.

"Alas, Crabbin's sense is that Herr Tree is not very good at heeding warnings."

"Maybe not so good," Tree agreed.

"Crabbin has a bad feeling. Herr Diavolo is a very dangerous man, perhaps Krampus himself."

34

It had begun to rain. A hard rain falling on the cobblestone square, drenching the statue of Joseph II on horseback, the Holy Roman Emperor forever leading the way. Tree was lost on rain-slicked Vienna streets deserted at this time of night, save for the shadow darting out of the square. Tree chased that shadow past massive baroque buildings.

The shadow formed into a black-clad figure disappearing into a narrow door in one of the buildings. Tree reached the open door and ducked inside.

A great hall with a coffered ceiling hung with chandeliers was surrounded by two tiers of spectator galleries. A passing rider in a black bicorn hat wearing a coffee-colored tunic, astride a white stallion, angrily yelled something in German. A dozen similarly dressed riders pranced around on white stallions. Somehow, Tree had stumbled into Vienna's legendary Spanish Riding School.

Another rider swept past, his horse's flank brushing against Tree, sending him sprawling onto the red-dirt floor.

"Careful, old man," Harry Lime said, bending to help Tree to his feet. "That's a Lipizzaner stallion. Their riders don't take kindly to you interfering when they're out for their morning practice."

Harry brushed the dirt off Tree before guiding him away from the prancing horses. "Really, old man, you shouldn't be following me around."

"I don't know what's going on," Tree said in a plaintive voice. "What am I doing here? What am I doing looking for a half-brother I don't even like while everyone mistakes me for him?"

"Don't you get it, old man?" Harry asked with an insouciant smile. "You are being played for what you're always been played for, the chump. You are the Holly Martins character in this story. You're trying to get the best of someone you cannot best, attempting to demonstrate your goodness against someone who does not value goodness and who threatens the secret that you've always kept from the world."

"I never said I was good, I never said I was anything," Tree protested. "All I'm trying to do is somehow get through."

"You are the boy-scout detective in shining armor. At least that's how you like to see yourself after reading too many of those ridiculous detective novels when you were a kid. The guy who is tempted but ends up always doing the right thing. Except there is someone who knows the darker part of you beneath that armor, the part you've never told your wife about, the part you've hidden from everyone—the part you're afraid he will reveal."

Tree looked around. The horses and their riders had disappeared. They were alone in the arena.

"We could cut you in, old man," Harry continued. "Make you part of it. What do they call it in the popular culture? The dark side? Except it's not all that dark. There is plenty of light, and it's very profitable, let me tell you. Come over and your secret is safe. Your brother would never betray a fellow traveler, now would he?"

"No," Tree cried, "I'm not like you and Scratch. I'm not. I'm not going to listen to you—"

"Tree, stop it." Freddie's voice calling out, echoing loudly off the coffered ceiling, shaking the chandeliers. What was she doing at the Spanish Riding School?

Except he was no longer at the riding school, he was sitting up in his own bed on Andy Rosse Lane on Captiva Island, Freddie hovering over him, that look of concern to which he had become all too accustomed.

"That's right," Tree said in a relieved voice. "We're home. We're not in Vienna anymore."

"Yes, Dorothy, you've been home safe and sound since yesterday afternoon. You were having another one of your dreams, that's all."

Thank goodness, he thought to himself as he hugged against Freddie, the relief washing through him. He wasn't Holly Martins, the hapless chump Harry Lime made him out to be.

Was he?

———

"It *is* a goldmine," Jerry Delson was saying to Rex Baxter as Tree joined them at the Bait Shack.

"Wait a minute," Tree said. "Isn't this where I left the two of you?"

"You mean at the point where I assured Rex his book is a goldmine?" Jerry said. "Hey, for your information, it's a goldmine."

"Except we haven't managed to find a publisher who wants to visit the mine." Rex did not sound very happy.

"The people who don't love the book, shouldn't *publish* the book," Jerry said. "We're looking for love, that's all. Once we find it—and believe me we will—hey, that's when the goldmine opens up."

He looked at Tree. "You look the worse for wear, Tree, if you don't mind my saying so."

"He's been in jail in Vienna," Rex said.

"There's a goddamn book here," Jerry said. "I keep saying it. If anyone should write a book it should be Tree Callister."

"Let's sell mine first," Rex said. "Besides, the local cops are looking for Tree. He's going to be in jail and not available for book deals."

"Let's view the situation from the bright side," Jerry said. "If he's in jail, he's gonna have plenty of time to write."

"That's you, Jerry," Rex said. "Always looking on the bright side."

"What can I tell you? I'm a bright-side kind of guy."

Rex didn't look convinced.

The Bait Shack was starting to fill with the luncheon crowd. Tree saw Gladys squeeze through and join them at the table. Tree watched Jerry's eyes light up.

Gladys ignored him. "The police are still looking for you," she said to Tree.

"And hello to you, too, Gladys," Tree said.

"The police are always looking for Tree," Rex grumbled.

"It's a book," Jerry Delson said.

"It feels good to be home," Tree said with a sigh.

Jerry cast another look in Gladys' direction and when she didn't respond, he turned his attention to his watch, announcing, "I've gotta get out of here."

"You've got a book to sell," Rex said.

"A three o'clock conference call. I'll be in touch," Jerry said, standing. "Just remember—"

"I know, I know," Rex said in a tired voice. "It's a goldmine."

"That's the spirit." Jerry beamed.

When Jerry was gone, Rex turned to Tree. "Tell us what happened."

"Did you find Scratch?" added Gladys.

"Found him. Lost him. Ended up in jail."

"The story of your life in a nutshell," Rex said.

A server brought Tree a Diet Coke as he recounted what happened after he and Freddie got to Vienna: Evka Bermann's denial that she was with Scratch; the encounter with Scratch at the Wiener Riesenrad; the discovery of the young Asian woman's body; Tree's subsequent arrest; the case of mistaken identity bolstered by the surprise appearance of Evka claiming that he was in fact Scratch.

"You and Scratch on the Ferris wheel in Vienna, right out of *The Third Man*," Rex said enthusiastically once Tree had finished. "I knew it. Scratch is Harry Lime, the devil himself. Unfortunately, Tree, you are poor, hapless Holly Martins."

"Harry Lime isn't the devil," Tree said.

"The devil in the flesh," Rex insisted. "Just like Scratch."

"Do you think he killed that woman?" Gladys asked.

"Scratch says he didn't," Tree said. "He claims he has powerful enemies who are trying to frame him."

"Do you believe him?" Gladys asked.

"He certainly has enemies," Tree said.

"This Vienna detective, Crabbin, what about him? It sounds as though he was actually working for Scratch."

"I'm not certain about Emile," Tree said. "I'm not certain about anything at this point. He turned out to be a bit of a chameleon."

"Not to mention Evka Bermann," Gladys said.

"Scratch conceded she had betrayed him."

"Did she?"

"Evka is at the top of the list of people I'm not sure about," Tree said.

"I repeat, welcome to the world of Tree Callister," Rex said.

"The Duckett brothers," Gladys said. "They're after Scratch. Who else?"

"Interpol. The police on two continents. Endless numbers of people are after Scratch. Like I say, he has enemies."

"Including you." Gladys, again.

"Yes, I guess you could add me to the list," Tree conceded.

"Which may be why he set you up so that it looked as though you killed that woman," Gladys said.

"But it was only a matter of time before the police realized I wasn't Scratch."

"That doesn't mean he didn't pin the murder on you, thinking that would give him enough time to get out of Vienna."

"Except, he got me out of there and made sure Crabbin drove Freddie and me to the airport."

"Could be he had second thoughts," Gladys suggested.

"I'm not sure Scratch has second thoughts," Tree said.

His cellphone began to make sounds. When he answered, Custer Duckett said, "Where are you, Mr. Callister?"

"I'm back in Florida," Tree said.

"It's time we had a talk," Custer said.

35

This time there was no terrace lunch and the Duckett brothers were not in their Speedos to greet Tree in a great room off the main entrance to their mansion. Today, they wore matching navy sports jackets, white slacks, and similar sour expressions.

In addition, if dirty looks could keep the Ducketts safe, then Lenny and Bob, Tree's two favorite toughs, were doing a terrific job. Once they had finished radiating disdain for Tree and made sure he didn't pose an imminent threat to the brothers, they disappeared.

"Frankly, Mr. Callister, we're disappointed," Custer Duckett said, sounding, well, disappointed.

"I'm sorry to hear that," Tree said.

"Considering the amount of money we paid you," Armstrong Duckett said.

"A great deal of money," Custer emphasized.

"Money for results," Armstrong added.

"At the least, we expected you to stay in contact more than you have," Custer said.

Armstrong said, "In fact, our view is that you didn't keep in contact at all."

"You sent me to Vienna to discover whether your wife was with Scratch," Tree said. "That's what I did."

"And also to get our money back," Custer said.

Armstrong cleared his throat and said, "The point is, we asked you here today in hopes you can provide us with better results."

"I'm not sure what that means," Tree said. "I did find Evka Bermann and I did speak to her."

"More to the point, I believe, she found you," Armstrong said.

"You were supposed to find out if she was with your brother," Custer said.

"My half-brother," Tree said. "Scratch was in Vienna, but I didn't see him with Evka. I think they had a falling out."

"What kind of falling out?"

"He believes Evka has betrayed him to the authorities in Vienna. That upset him. At this point, I would have to say they are not together."

The Duckett brothers exchanged glances. "But he still lied to us and therefore in our view of it, stole our money," Armstrong said.

"However, if in fact they are no longer together that must factor into any decisions you make concerning the future of your marriage," Custer said to Armstrong.

"You're still hoping to save your marriage?" Tree couldn't believe what he was hearing.

"I am open to discussions on the matter," Armstrong said.

Custer shook his head. "I've attempted many times to talk sense into my brother. I cannot believe he's even entertaining the idea of any sort of reconciliation with that woman."

"It's my damned business, my damned life," Armstrong flared.

"You are a fool," Custer said.

"To hell with you," Armstrong said.

"I will meet you there," Custer snapped. "Because hell is exactly where you are headed if you continue to pursue that woman."

"She is not *that woman*," Armstrong yelled. "She is my *wife*!"

Both brothers were reduced to silence during which they traded hostile looks.

"For what it's worth," Tree finally interjected. "When I spoke to her, she was pretty adamant about ending the marriage."

"I have spoken to her, and I get a different sense," Armstrong said.

"What Callister is telling us, that sounds pretty certain to me," Custer said.

"Not to me it doesn't," insisted Armstrong.

"I can only tell you what Evka told me." He addressed Armstrong. "She said that no matter what, your marriage is over. She isn't coming back."

"I told you," Custer said in an accusatory voice.

"You told me *nothing*," Armstrong snapped. "You never wanted us to be together."

"It might have had something to do with the fact that you ran off with my wife."

"I didn't *run* off with her, as you say. We stayed right here."

"And screwed under my goddamn nose." Custer's voice had angrily risen several decibels.

"Hey," Tree said with a force that made the brothers jerk to attention. "This isn't doing us any good. I'm sorry the news isn't better but you're paying me to be honest and this is what it is."

"No, it isn't," Armstrong stated.

Custer shot him a look. "What are you getting at?"

"I want Mr. Callister to find my wife."

"That's ridiculous," Custer said. "You heard him. She doesn't want anything to do with you."

"It's because of that bastard. He's cast some sort of spell on her. She's not herself, not thinking straight." Armstrong addressed Tree. "Find her for me, please, and when you do, I will take it from there."

"A waste of money," pronounced Custer.

"I have no idea where to look for her," Tree said. "For all I know she's still in Vienna."

"No." Armstrong vehemently shook his head. "She's back here."

"How do you know that?" Custer demanded.

"I spoke to her this morning. She said she had returned from Vienna."

"Then you know where she is," Tree offered.

"She wouldn't tell me," Armstrong said. "I don't want arguments. Do it. I will make it worth your while, Mr. Callister."

"If we are to engage this insanity, I have a further request," Custer stated.

"And what is that?" demanded Armstrong.

Custer turned to Tree. "The whereabouts of your brother."

"Half-brother," Tree said.

"He stole a great deal of money from us," Custer said. "I still want it returned."

"His argument will be that he has lived up to the agreement he made with you," Tree said.

"Just find him," Custer said. "We will take care of the rest."

"I'm going to have to deal with the fact that Scratch believes Evka is working with people who were trying to frame him for a murder in Vienna, do either of you know anything about that?"

"Your brother is a duplicitous, lying criminal and a possible murderer to boot," Custer said. "I wouldn't believe a word out of his mouth."

"If I suspected BlackHeart was somehow involved in all this, what would you say?"

"I would say find Armstrong's wife and locate Scratch," Custer said curtly. "We have no interest in anything else."

"And what if I don't want to take on either of these jobs?"

"Saying no to us is not a good idea, Mr. Callister," Custer said. "We are willing to pay you a lot more money. It will certainly be worth your while. In return you will have helped us a great deal and, even better, you will not have made enemies of us."

"Because, Mr. Callister," Armstrong added, "you do not want us as enemies."

He did not smile when he said it.

36

Tree came off Fort Myers Beach onto San Carlos Boulevard, questioning yet again how he had managed to get himself into a mess with no idea how he was going to get out of it. For the life of him, he couldn't figure out how he did it. But he always managed.

His cellphone sounded. It was Freddie.

"Where are you?"

"On San Carlos on my way home," Tree said.

"Don't come home," she said.

"Why not?"

"The police are here with a search warrant."

"What are they saying?"

"They want to know where you are."

"In connection with what?"

"There are a variety of topics, of course. But I believe they are interested in the late Albert Aberfoyle."

Damn, Tree thought. He had almost forgotten about the murdered Albert Aberfoyle aka Winston Dyab.

"I'll talk to you later," Tree said.

"What are you going to do?"

"As usual, I'm not sure."

"Be careful," Freddie said.

He had no sooner hung up from Freddie than his cellphone sounded again. This time it was Gladys.

"Don't come to the office," she said.

"Don't tell me. The police are there."

"With a search warrant. How did you guess?"

"Hey, I'm a trained private investigator," Tree said.

"Rex tried to warn me, but even I had no idea how much shit you can keep getting yourself into," Gladys said.

"Are you at the office?"

"Standing outside. They threw us out. Listen, I've been doing some research into this BlackHeart."

"Tell me," Tree said.

"Okay, confusion, confrontation, disruption, that's their motto, fine. But then what? I asked myself. What do these guys actually *do*?"

"And how does my half-brother fit in with them?"

"Exactly," said Gladys. "The web site says the Duckett brothers are the founders of BlackHeart, but I don't think they are. I think it's a guy named Lobo Salvador."

The Watcher, Tree thought.

Lobo late at night by firelight off a deserted highway, Tree remembered. Lobo, the magic man, rescuing him. Lobo now causing him to shudder slightly.

The Watcher watching.

"Tree, are you there?"

"Yes," he said.

"You know who this guy is?"

"There's a photograph of him on the website," Tree said.

"If there was, it's not there anymore," Gladys said.

"It was there, I saw it. The Watcher. If I'm right he's leading a group dedicated to spreading sin and corruption."

"I would have said sin and corruption don't need any help. They do just fine on their own. But whoever this guy Lobo is, he's never in one place long, keeps moving around, flying pretty much under the radar."

"See if you can find out where he is now," Tree said.

"Gotta go," Gladys said quickly. "They're coming out."

Gladys hung up.

Tree drove to Port Comfort Road, turned right and parked at the Lighthouse Restaurant. The bar was quiet at this time of the afternoon. Tree sat at one end and ordered a Diet Coke and a grouper sandwich. He pulled out his cellphone and looked up the number that almost immediately produced the angry voice of Detective Cee Jay Boone.

"Where the hell are you?" she demanded.

"Everyone wants to know where I am," Tree said. "I've never felt so popular."

"There is a warrant out for your arrest," Cee Jay said.

"Come on, Cee Jay, you can't really believe I had anything to do with Albert Aberfoyle's murder."

"You mean Winston Dyab."

"I make it a habit never to kill a client whose name I can't get right."

"Why don't you tell me where you are, Tree, and then we can talk about it."

"As I always say, I'm more than happy to cooperate with law enforcement but first of all, I need your help with something."

"For Christ's sake, I'm trying to arrest you, Tree, not help you." Cee Jay sounded exasperated.

"I need you to get me any information you may have on a guy named Lobo Salvador."

Cee Jay paused a bit too long before she said, "Why would you be interested in him?"

"Then you know who he is."

"I repeat: why are you interested?"

"Tell you what," Tree said. "Meet with me, tell me what you know about Lobo Salvador, and then you can arrest me to your heart's content."

Cee Jay hesitated some more before she said, "Where are you?"

"The Lighthouse Restaurant on Port Comfort Road."

Shortly after Cee Jay hung up on him, his grouper sandwich arrived. They did a terrific grouper sandwich at the Lighthouse. Tree wondered if it would be the last good meal he would have for a while. He knew for a fact that the grouper sandwiches at the Lee County Jail weren't nearly as good.

37

Tree wasn't sure if Cee Jay would come through the door at the Lighthouse with a SWAT team or a smile. She came with a frown—the expression she usually adopted when dealing with Tree.

"You timed it perfectly," Tree said as she eased herself on the stool beside him. "I just finished my grouper sandwich. Are you hungry? They do a very good grouper sandwich here."

"I don't want a grouper sandwich," Cee Jay said.

"You can't be bribed with a grouper sandwich, is that it?"

"I want you to come with me."

"First, tell me about Lobo Salvador."

"I don't have to tell you shit," she said.

"Look, I know about BlackHeart. I'm doing some work for the Duckett brothers."

That actually appeared to capture Cee Jay's interest. "What kind of work?"

"His wife left one of the brothers. They want me to find her."

"Which brother?"

"Depends," Tree said. "Custer married Evka first. She divorced him and married Armstrong."

"You're kidding." Cee Jay looked genuinely surprised.

"Now Evka has left Armstrong. I followed her to Vienna. I think she's back here. You see? I haven't had time to kill anyone this week."

"As you know because you were at the scene, Winston Dyab, aka Albert Aberfoyle, wasn't killed this week."

"He paid me a lot of money. Why would I kill him?"

"We've been in touch with the New Orleans police. They tell us Aberfoyle or Dyab, in addition to the Ponzi scheme he was running locally, was searching for a man named Carl Chamuco, aka Patrick Diavolo, aka Samuel Callister—your brother."

"My half-brother," Tree said.

"You murdered him to protect your brother."

"I wouldn't kill anyone, let alone do it to protect Scratch," Tree said.

"Then come in and convince me and the other investigating officers, because right now a lot of people think you look pretty good for this."

"A lot of people sounds suspiciously like my good friend, Detective Owen Markfield."

"He could well be one of those people."

"Tell me what you know about Lobo Salvador and BlackHeart."

Cee Jay looked puzzled. "BlackHeart?"

"Or the Watcher? Do those names mean anything to you?"

"I know Salvador because we got a request a couple of weeks ago from Interpol seeking information about him. Also, anything we knew about Lobo and a female companion."

"What female companion?"

"A woman named Jana Teufel." When she saw the look on Tree's face, Cee Jay asked, "Do you know her?"

"Jana Teufel also goes under the name of Evka Bermann," Tree said.

"Is that why you're interested in Salvador?"

"It is now," Tree said. "Did Interpol say why they wanted him?"

"Apparently, Lobo has been moving around Europe collecting millions by telling people who should know better that he can save them from the devil."

"What's wrong with that?"

"Nothing, unless you start making people disappear who don't pay up."

"Is that what he's doing?"

"That's what Interpol believes he is doing."

"With BlackHeart."

"Interpol didn't mention anything about BlackHeart— or this Watcher thing. What's that?"

"Lobo is known as the Watcher. I believe he founded BlackHeart and from what you're telling me, he's using that organization to defraud people."

"Okay, I suppose that's helpful," Cee Jay said without enthusiasm. "Now let's get out of here."

"Do you know where Lobo is?"

"Interpol believe he is somewhere in the Lee County area. They say he flew out of Vienna with Jana Teufel to Berlin."

"You're sure it was Vienna?"

"According to Interpol. From there, they got on a Lufthansa flight that landed at Fort Myers International Airport."

"Thanks for this, Cee Jay."

"Have you paid for your grouper sandwich?"

"Why do you ask?"

"Because," Cee Jay said, throwing a pair of handcuffs on the countertop, "you're under arrest."

A voice covered in honey announced: "It looks as though I have arrived, as they used to say in the westerns I grew up with, in the nick of time."

Simultaneously Cee Jay and Tree turned to see T. Emmett Hawkins, resplendent in bow tie, the full force of that honeyed Georgia drawl on display, his reassuring smile seeming to say 'you are innocent and I will prove it.' It was the smile that had gotten Tree out of many jams; the smile at work this afternoon.

"You've met my attorney, the more-than-honorable T. Emmett Hawkins," Tree said.

In contrast to the sunniness of Hawkins' smile, Cee Jay's frown was deep as she picked the handcuffs up off the counter.

38

"A fishing expedition," pronounced T. Emmett Hawkins as they emerged two hours later from Sanibel Police Headquarters. "As so often happens with you, Tree, they want to believe you are guilty of a crime like murder, but they don't really believe it. In the meantime, it's worth their while to make your life as miserable as they possibly can."

"I don't think they like me," Tree said.

"That's a view I would not disagree with," Hawkins said mildly.

"Well, thanks for being here, Emmett."

"You know, my late predecessor as your attorney used to say that you were a man born to spend the rest of his life in jail."

"Funny," Tree said, "until about twelve years ago, I never thought twice about the possibility of jail. I was as close to a model citizen as you can get."

"And now?"

"Almost everywhere I go, someone either puts me in jail or threatens to put me in jail."

"You did retire for a time," Hawkins said.

"I got drawn back into it," Tree said.

"Yes, well, far be it for me to be handing out advice, but if you asked, I'd suggest you reconsider that retirement."

"You sound like Freddie," Tree said.

"In addition to being one of our great beauties, Freddie is also a woman possessed of infinite good sense."

"Yet she's married to a man with absolutely no sense at all," Tree said.

"Well, at least you recognize your shortcomings, Tree. Not that it does much good, unfortunately."

The two men shook hands. "It's good to see you, Emmett. Thanks."

Hawkins chuckled and said, "It's *never* good when you see me, Tree. But hopefully it is at least helpful when it comes to keeping you out of jail."

"Or getting me out of jail once I'm in."

"Listen to your lovely wife," Hawkins said as he went off. "Consider retirement."

"Emmett thinks you're one of the great beauties not to mention a person with infinite good sense," Tree said once he was home and he and Freddie had retreated to the terrace and the sound of happy tourists enjoying the sunset down the street at the Mucky Duck.

"Emmett, in addition to being the best Tree Callister get-out-of-jail card around, is a sweetheart."

"He also thinks I should think about retiring,"

"What did you say to that idea?" Freddie placed her wine glass on the table.

"I said he sounded like my wife."

"This may come as a surprise, but most people visit Vienna without seeing the inside of a police station. The majority of residents on Captiva never see a policeman let alone have their house searched."

"I did manage to pull some information out of Cee Jay Boone," Tree said.

"What information?"

"Interpol is looking for Lobo Salvador who, according to what Gladys has been able to uncover, is the founder of BlackHeart, not, as I thought, the Duckett brothers."

"The same Lobo you met when you drove my car off the road."

"When I swerved so I wouldn't kill a black panther, an endangered species. But yes, the same guy who mysteriously got the car started when I couldn't."

"What's Interpol's interest in him?"

"They want him for questioning in connection with an extortion scheme they think he is running."

"This saint-like figure you encountered."

"That's the point. Apparently, he has been extorting money from people, claiming he can save them from the devil."

"Seriously?"

"And if they don't pay up, his victims tend to disappear."

"Okay, but other than the fact you suspect Scratch is the devil himself, how does Lobo fit into all this?"

"Maybe Scratch isn't the devil. Maybe the devil is the Watcher—Lobo Salvador. Forgetting for the time being that there is no such thing as the devil."

"You obviously didn't read *Rosemary's Baby* or *The Exorcist*," Freddie said.

"Be that as it may, Interpol says Lobo recently left Vienna with a woman named Jana Teufel."

"Also known as Evka Bermann," Freddie said. "But then where *is* Evka and her boyfriend, Lobo?"

"That's what I have to find out," Tree said.

"You're going up against the devil, is that it?" Freddie said.

"It's like I said."

"Remind me," Freddie said.

"There's no such thing as the devil."

39

The next morning, Tree phoned Gladys and had her pick him up in her new truck. They drove out to Fort Myers Beach, along Estero Boulevard. When Gladys began to suspect where they were headed, she said, "Isn't this where the Duckett brothers live?"

"That's right, Gladys," Tree said, impressed. "You've done your homework."

"It's not like I didn't get plenty of experience with this shit in Los Angeles," Gladys said. "But I do have a question."

"What's that?"

"These guys hired you, right?"

"That's right."

"Then what are we doing staking out their place?"

"Is that what you think we're doing?"

"Tell me something different," Gladys said. "You've got me driving in case they recognize you. The question is, why are you doing this?"

"Because something's not right," Tree said. "I'm not sure what it is, but something. Let's see."

"You got it," Gladys said.

Once they passed the Santini Mall, Tree directed Gladys to turn off Estero onto Black Island and Palm Tree Lane where the Duckett estate was located.

"Pull over just past the gate," Tree said.

Once Gladys had parked, Tree got into the back seat so he could keep an eye on the Duckett gate. The Florida heat rose around them, accompanied by the sound of cicadas. Otherwise, silence.

"I love staking out the rich," Gladys said. "They're all so quiet. You'd think they'd play loud music or something. But they never do."

She twisted around to Tree. "There's a cooler right behind you. You mind pulling it up for me?"

He wrestled the yellow portable cooler over the back of the seat and then pushed it forward to Gladys who set it beside her. She took the lid off and Tree saw that it was full of beer cans. "You want one?" Gladys asked.

"No thanks," Tree said.

"You mind?" She lifted the can in her hand.

Tree shook his head, the signal for Gladys to snap the tab and take a long drink. "That's better," she said. "Can I tell you something that stays between the two of us?"

"Sure," Tree said.

"I'm a little worried about Rex."

That surprised Tree. "Rex? What about him?"

"He's crazy about me," Gladys said. "He wants to date me."

"I wondered if something was going on," Tree said.

"I mean, I like Rex, but, like how old is that dude? He slept with Joan Crawford, for God's sake."

"Well, Joan was pretty old at the time and Rex was very young."

"Even so," Gladys said. "Besides, it's the workplace, right? We should be keeping it professional."

"Yes, we should," Tree said. "Would you like me to talk to him?"

Gladys considered this, taking another drink from her beer. "Let it go for now. I just wanted you to know what was going down in case you get the wrong impression about me."

"You mean beyond you drinking beer at eleven o'clock in the morning?"

Gladys grinned. "Well, you know I'm a badass, Tree. And you wouldn't want it any other way, would you?"

"Just what we need at the office," Tree said. "A badass receptionist."

"One of these days I will actually answer the phone," Gladys said. "Of course, it would help if the phone rings."

"What about Jerry Delson? He seems to light up every time he sees you."

"Men just can't keep their hands off me, what can I say?"

"Apparently not," Tree said.

"I like Jerry. He's a character. He wants me to write a book."

"Jerry wants everyone he meets to write a book," Tree said.

Gladys issued a burst of laughter and shook her head. "Ain't it the truth? I told him I slept with Bob Hope."

"No kidding," Tree said. "How old was Bob when that happened?"

"Not so old, as it turned out," Gladys said with a grin.

"Are you going to write a book?"

"Rex can write a book. You can write a book. I can write a book. We can sit around the office at the Cattle Dock Bait Company writing books all day long. The question is, can Jerry sell them?"

"Goldmines," Tree said.

"Yeah, right," Gladys said. "Jerry seems to have trouble finding that elusive goldmine."

An hour later, as Tree fought to stop himself from dozing off, it was Gladys who noticed the Range Rover coming out of the Duckett residence heading toward Estero Boulevard.

"That's Armstrong," Tree said as Gladys started the motor and swung the truck around. By the time she got to the corner, the Range Rover had turned onto Estero.

The Range Rover proceeded to Hickory Island where Estero became Hickory Boulevard. The road swung left and turned into Bonita Beach Road. Armstrong followed it to Old 41 Road and made a left.

"Any idea where we are?" Gladys asked, keeping her eyes firmly on the Range Rover ahead.

"Bonita Springs," Tree said.

Armstrong crossed a bridge over a narrow river and then promptly turned off into the parking area for Everglades Wonder Gardens. As they drove past, Tree saw Armstrong stopped in front of a low building with a wide porch and a big Entrance sign on its roof.

Gladys parked around the corner and turned off the engine. "Now what?"

"Let's go inside," Tree said. "He doesn't know you, so I'll hang back while you take the lead."

"Roger that." Gladys opened her door and got out.

She followed Tree around to the front. They climbed the steps to the porch that ran the length of the building and went inside. Tree paid the entrance fee and they stepped out to a pathway winding through banyan trees crowded with visitors admiring the ibis strutting among peafowl and ducks unperturbed by all the attention.

Further on, bright orange flamingos crowded the shore of a lagoon, preening themselves, gracefully accepting the kibble offered in small cups. Gladys appeared transfixed by the scene. Tree caught sight of Armstrong, ignoring a gaggle of peacocks shuttling out of the way so he could push by.

Tree hurried forward as Armstrong passed a fenced-in area containing, according to the sign, the "world's largest collection" of alligators. The sulcata tortoise display was similarly ignored as Armstrong disappeared around an imposing stand of banyan trees. Tree reached the end of the path. An elegant wrought-iron gazebo seemed out of place amid the wildlife splendors of the Wonder Gardens. Inside, tables were covered with white linen, laid with formal china and silverware, everything ready should Renoir turn up to paint the scene. Instead of Renoir, however, there was Armstrong Duckett seated at the far end, checking his watch.

Tree looked around. There was no sign of Gladys. A peacock swayed past, followed by a small girl and boy anxious for a closer look.

Tree turned to let them pass and nearly missed Evka Bermann as she entered the gazebo. She was back in Florida, dazzling in a short white skirt and top. Armstrong, stumbling to his feet, appeared suitably awed. If there was an exhibit of Lovesick Fools at the Everglades Wonder Gardens, Armstrong would be a suitable addition.

"Why don't we allow the lovebirds to have privacy?"

Lobo Salvador wearing a smile and dressed in black, stood behind him.

40

Supposing I don't want to give them any privacy," Tree said. "Supposing I want to ask the two of them what the hell is going on."

"Look, I know it's unnecessary to say this, but we have your friend outside," Lobo said gently. "She is, shall we say, feisty, eh? A character."

"Don't harm her," Tree said tightly.

"Of course not. Last thing I desire. Come along and we have a talk, how's that?"

As he was the night Tree met him, Lobo was dressed in black, his black hair swept back to fall neatly to his shoulders, the same thin beard growth. Amid the splendor of the Wonder Gardens he gave off the sense of a pirate who had lost his ship. The gentle smile offered comfort. Then how was it, Tree wondered, that he felt so uncomfortable? The Watcher watching him too closely? Maybe that was it.

"Why not?" Tree said with a shrug.

"There's a bench by the lagoon. We can feed the flamingos."

"I don't want to feed the flamingos."

"Sure you do," Lobo insisted. "No one can resist the beauty of the flamingos."

Tree followed Lobo to an empty bench beside the lagoon. Flamingos moved on spindly legs to gather around him as he produced a cup of kibble. The birds took turns poking into the cup with their long beaks.

"I am not sure about these pellets," Lobo said, keeping an eye on one of the birds posing in the water, spreading its wings. "They supposedly contain the nutrients that allow the birds to retain their bright colors. And the food is placed in the water so they can continue to use their filtering systems to eat. But it can't be the same as in the wild can it?"

"Your concern for flamingos is heartfelt I'm sure," Tree said, "but then there is a dead man on Sanibel and a murdered woman in Vienna, and I wonder if the Watcher has the same concern for them."

"Watcher?" Lobo blessed his question with another gentle smile. He concentrated on the flamingos, saying nothing.

Finally, the cup was empty. Lobo sighed, looking down at it with a sad expression. He said, "We should talk about your brother."

"I don't have a brother," Tree said. "I have a half-brother."

"Whatever you care to call him, Scratch has a great deal to answer for."

"Does he?"

"I imagine he is why you are doing what you are doing. It has nothing to do with Evka or the Duckett brothers. You could care less about them; it is your brother you want."

"Well, for one thing, the Ducketts want their three million dollars back."

Lobo gave a shrug. "I tried to warn you about Scratch when we first met."

"What? Scratch is the devil?" Tree's voice was full of disdain. "The way I hear it, when it comes to candidates for devilry, you're at the top of the list. The head of BlackHeart, the Watcher dedicated to spreading sin and corruption."

Lobo took his eyes off the flamingos and focused on Tree. "Your brother has become a problem for me and for my organization."

"You are talking about BlackHeart."

"That's one name for it, I suppose."

"The Watchers could be another. But BlackHeart is the name the Ducketts use."

"The Ducketts follow their way, but it is not always my way."

"Or Scratch's, I'm guessing."

"He has become a renegade, an agent pursuing his own darkness. We have tried to stop him, but, as you might guess, he is not easily stopped."

Tree didn't say anything.

"I know that when you were children, you were present when he was hit by lightning on Sanibel. That changed everything. You know that better than anyone."

"I know what Scratch likes to think," Tree said.

Lobo threw up his hands, an unexpected gesture of impatience. "You're in denial. And yet at the same time you relentlessly seek out your brother. The fascinating thing about you, Tree, I can't tell whether you want him to live or die."

"You don't know anything about what I want or don't want," Tree said.

"Don't I?" Lobo allowed the question to hang in the air.

"What are you getting at?" Tree demanded. "What's this all about?"

Lobo stood, holding the now-empty cup. "I asked you whether you wanted Scratch to live or die. You didn't answer me."

"Suppose I said I want him alive."

"Then it will be up to you to ensure that happens. Defend him properly and he lives. Fail to defend him and he dies."

"I don't know what you're talking about."

"Your search for Scratch is over. He is with us. There is no need for you to keep looking for him."

"Tell me where he is."

"I will be in touch. We will meet again. That's when all this will be resolved. Until then, please leave the Ducketts and their family problems alone. They will not get you Scratch. Only I can do that."

He handed Tree the cup. Now it was full of pellets.

"Feed the flamingos," Lobo said. "They are always hungry."

Tree looked at the cup in his hand, hiding his surprise. "There is one other possibility."

"Yes?"

"You and your group killed Albert Aberfoyle and Kim Rada, and have framed Scratch for the murders."

"Make sure you bring that up at his trial," Lobo said.

"Trial?" Tree said, confused.

But Lobo was gone.

41

Outside, Tree found Gladys leaning against the hood of the truck, smoking a cigarette.

"I thought you quit smoking."

"That was before I got involved with you again," she said. "And here I thought I was going to be a receptionist for a bestselling author. The easy life in Florida. Ha!"

"Are you all right?"

"I'd be better if two goons hadn't taken me by surprise in there. I would be a whole lot better if I could have gotten to my gun in the glove compartment."

"Probably just as well," Tree said. "The flamingos don't like guns."

"They're Florida flamingos, they're used to guns." She finished her cigarette. "I was worried about you."

"I'm okay," Tree said. "Lobo just wanted to talk."

"Lobo Salvador? The guy behind BlackHeart?"

"He says that's one name for it," Tree said.

"Jesus H. Christ," Gladys said, throwing her cigarette away. "Who is that guy?"

"God or the devil, I'm not sure which."

"My money is on the devil," Gladys said. "Or the devil's disciple—the Watcher."

"I think he believes that position is occupied by Scratch."

Around the corner, Gladys noticed familiar movement at the Wonder Gardens entrance. Armstrong Duckett, exiting the complex, head down.

Alone.

"What happened to Evka Bermann?" Freddie asked after Tree got home and told her of the day's events at the Everglades Wonder Gardens.

"No sign of her," Tree said. "She must have left by another exit."

"The elusive Evka," Freddie said. "There, but never quite there, here, or in Vienna."

"I'm not sure she has much to do with this other than to play the role of estranged wife of the Ducketts and lover for Scratch Callister and maybe Lobo Salvador, too."

"I don't know about that," Freddie countered. "I think she's the key to this whole thing."

"Evka?"

"Or Jana Teufel. Take your pick of the names for these people. Whatever this whole thing turns out to be, which, at the moment, I must concede, has me mystified."

"Okay, here's what we know," Tree said. "BlackHeart is this shadowy international organization founded by the mysterious Watcher, Lobo Salvador, funded by the Duckett brothers, if I'm not mistaken. The Ducketts are sort of the front for the organization. Somehow, Scratch got involved with them. I believe this was one of the cons he managed to pull with various suckers, including the late Albert Aberfoyle. He somehow convinced the BlackHeart people he possessed dark powers, and of course they liked that idea."

"Powers he doesn't have?"

"Of course not," Tree said. "Scratch has the ability to pull the wool over the eyes of dangerous people he shouldn't be involved with in the first place and keep getting himself into trouble as a result. As far as being the spawn of the devil or something like that, no."

"So where does that leave us?" Freddie asked.

"Lobo says I don't have to look for Scratch anymore. They have him."

"They being BlackHeart."

"Yes."

"And what are they going to do with him?"

"That's what worries me. Lobo said something about a trial."

"What kind of trial?"

"I have no idea. Lobo said he would be in touch."

"I'm still confused about BlackHeart. Who and what are they? The devil's disciples?"

"Maybe they like to think they are," Tree said.

"But?"

"But there's no such thing as the devil."

"That's what we keep telling ourselves," Freddie said.

Tree rolled his eyes. "Come on, Freddie. What? You think there is?"

"The jury appears to be out on that matter," Freddie replied carefully. "And what about our friend, Evka, aka Jana Teufel."

"I don't think she's the devil, either," Tree said.

"I don't know about that," Freddie said. "Maybe…"

"What?"

"The devil is a woman." As she said this, Freddie made a drama out of raising and then lowering her eyebrows.

42

Freddie signaled the lateness of the hour with an impressive series of yawns. Time for bed, she announced. Tree said he would be there in a few minutes. He wanted to check his email. But he didn't really want to check his email. What he needed was time to think, although he had to concede his history of thinking did not usually produce great results.

He went out and down the steps to the terrace. The stars were out over Captiva. The moon was nearly full. He could hear the soft sound of the waves at the beach. A perfect Florida night with just enough of a breeze to keep the humidity away.

Tree thought about Scratch and Evka Bermann and Lobo Salvador, the Watcher who could scare you away with his sense of danger and at the same time draw you in with his charisma. An uneasy combination. He thought of Freddie's suspicions about Evka and all the questions swirling around in his mind. The answers were not easily available and yet the questions continued to nag at him. If he waited for Lobo Salvador, who knew what he might encounter? More immediate answers might be available from the Ducketts—the brothers who had sent him in search of a woman Armstrong Duckett had no trouble finding; the Ducketts whose time had come to stop bullshitting and give him some straight answers.

He went into the bedroom. Freddie was sound asleep. He went outside to the Mercedes. This was the part in movies he could never buy, the moment when the husband sneaks out of bed, doesn't wake the wife, and goes off into the night in pursuit of the next plot twist; the wife never wakes up and never asks questions.

Well, here he was sneaking out in the night without telling his wife; he would never buy it if he were watching the movie, but here he was doing it. Life, he decided, as he started the car, does on occasion imitate bad movies.

Well, his life, anyway.

———

By the time he reached Black Island almost an hour later, Tree was beginning to have second—third?—thoughts. It was almost midnight. The Ducketts would probably be in bed by now. But as he approached the house, he could see lights glimmering through the massive foliage. To his surprise, the entrance gate was wide open.

He parked on the shoulder across from the entrance. He walked toward the house feeling the beginnings of all-too-familiar unease. He reached the front door and rang the bell. He could hear the sound echo through the house, but no one came. He tried the latch and found the door unlocked. He pushed it open and stepped into a darkened hallway. A single light came from somewhere deeper in the house.

"Hello," Tree called out. "It's Tree Callister. Hello?"

No answer. Tree had another familiar feeling—the tightening in his stomach followed by an overwhelming sense of dread.

The first bullet whistled past his ear and smacked into the wall behind him almost before he heard the weak pop of the gun firing. Instinctively, he ducked down trying to see through the gloom. A figure darted in and out of view at the end of the hall as there was a second pop, the bullet ricocheting off the newel post on a nearby banister.

Tree retreated up the staircase, exactly the wrong direction in which he should be retreating, he thought fleetingly. He was halfway up the stairs when the explosion shook the house, throwing him against the wall.

The explosion was immediately followed by a pall of choking smoke. Tree reached the second floor. He glanced back down the stairwell and saw only more smoke and flames. He hurried along the hall, looking for another way back down and out of what was now a burning house. He burst through the open double doors at the end of the hall and found himself in a sprawling master bedroom. Armstrong Duckett sat naked in an armchair stained with the blood flowing out of the chest and abdomen where he had been shot.

As Tree approached, Armstrong moved and his eyes fluttered open as though to acknowledge Tree's presence. He leaned down to him, saying, "Armstrong, who did this?"

Armstrong's lips moved. He tried to speak but the words wouldn't come out.

"Armstrong," Tree repeated.

"I...," Armstrong managed, and then, "Loved her... always...loved her."

His eyes glazed over and he stopped breathing.

Tree heard a scream behind him and suddenly Custer was in the room, swathed in flames but still managing to wave around the gun he held in his hand. He fired it into the air as he screamed once more and then collapsed to his knees.

Tree watched in horror as Custer dropped the gun and fell forward, writhing on the carpet. Tree grabbed the duvet off the nearby bed and used it to smother the flames. But it was too late. By now the room had filled with smoke and flames moving at extraordinary speed, an invading force coming for Tree. He stumbled to his feet, choking, fighting for breath, looking for a way out when there seemed to be no way out.

On the far side of the room, through the thickening smoke, Tree spotted a pair of French doors. He lurched across, fumbled with the latch and got the door open and fell out onto a balcony that overlooked a swimming pool. Tree leaned against the balustrade, inhaling the night air, clearing his head. Behind him, a curtain of fire advanced.

"Shit," Tree announced to the night. The night, as it tended to do, paid no attention. He lifted himself onto the balustrade and looked down at the pool. It wasn't that far, he consoled himself. Except, shit, it *was* that far. He maneuvered himself so that he was seated atop the balustrade, his feet dangling over. Was that the pool's deep end below? Was there even a deep end? And supposing there wasn't a deep end? A lot of pools these days, he recalled, were built with no deep end. Hadn't he read that somewhere? But the Ducketts were rich. Surely, they could afford a deep end.

There was, he decided, one way to find out.

He closed his eyes and pushed himself out into as close an approximation of the wild blue yonder as he ever hoped to push himself into.

Tree hit the water feet-first. He went under, his feet hitting bottom before he bounced up, breaking the surface. Above him, the smoke and fire poured onto the terrace and the roof erupted in flames, dropping debris into the pool and onto the pool deck.

Tree pushed across to the other side and then lifted himself out of the water. He lay on the pool deck, soaking wet, breathing hard, amazed—and relieved—that he had not broken every bone in his body.

A high wall surrounded the pool. At the far end, a door was recessed into the wall. Tree gathered what strength he had left and with difficulty got to his feet. Pain shot down his thigh. His sciatic nerve did not take kindly to late night pool dives. He limped over to the door. It opened onto the driveway. He was halfway down the drive when there was a second explosion. Tree turned as the roof began to collapse and the whole house was ablaze, lighting up the night—hellfire, Tree couldn't help thinking.

As he stood there, a car careened into view coming around from the front of the house. It picked up speed as it came at Tree. He had a moment to jump out of the way as the car swerved past and he caught a glimpse of Evka Bermann's intense profile. Then the car disappeared out the front gate.

Maybe Freddie was right, Tree thought. Maybe the devil *was* a woman.

43

"B y the time I got to my car and started after her, she had disappeared," Tree explained to Freddie when he got home, waking her up, a bedraggled figure, still damp from his dip in the Duckett brothers' swimming pool.

"But you're sure it was Evka," Freddie said.

"It was Evka all right," Tree said, stripping off his wet clothes.

"She set the house on fire and murdered Custer and Armstrong Duckett," Freddie said decisively.

"Or contrarily, someone came into the house, set off an explosion that started the fire, and killed the Ducketts. But Evka managed to escape."

"That would mean Evka had returned to the marital bed," Freddie said. "Unlikely, if you ask me. Remember what I said."

"Your suggestion that the devil is a woman."

"That's the one," Freddie said.

"It did cross my mind as Evka drove past me," Tree admitted.

"You didn't stick around for the police," Freddie said.

"Right now, the fewer people who know I was there, the better."

"Except Evka knows."

Tree shrugged. "I'm not sure if she saw me."

"But someone shot at you," Freddie said.

"That was probably Custer. He had the gun."

"You should have waited for the police," Freddie said.

"I knew you were going to say that."

"This is getting crazier and crazier and once again my husband finds himself right where I don't want him to be."

"Where is that?"

"In over your head."

"Yes, a not unfamiliar place."

"Tree, you almost got yourself killed tonight."

"It's not like I drove out there intending to get killed," Tree protested.

"That's another thing. You left without saying a word. You think you're in one of those movies where the protagonist leaves in the middle of the night and the wife remains sound asleep."

"I didn't want to wake you," Tree said.

"Well, you did wake me, but by the time I got out of bed you were gone. Of course, knowing I would call, you didn't take your cellphone."

"I forgot it, that's all." Which was sort of true, he told himself.

Freddie threw up her hands in exasperation. "So now what?"

"We wait for Lobo to get in touch, I suppose."

"I guess we can be certain of one thing tonight," Freddie said.

"What's that?"

"If Lobo really is holding Scratch, then Scratch couldn't have had anything to do with what happened at the Duckett house."

"I hope you're right."

"Which makes me wonder about the murders of Albert Aberfoyle and Kim Rada."

"You suspect Evka," Tree said.

"She seems to be around every time someone ends up dead," Freddie pointed out.

Tree lay on the bed beside Freddie. "I should take a shower," he said.

"You're changing the subject," Freddie said.

"I'm too tired to change anything."

Freddie snuggled against him. "A difficult day at the office."

"Day and night," Tree murmured. "My work is never done."

"It's tough being the hero of your own life," Freddie said.

Tree didn't answer. He had begun to snore gently.

––––––––

The world engulfed in flames, Tree racing through fire, running for his life, the black panther leaping out of the conflagration, its eyes bright yellow spotlights, Tree freezing, the panther crouching, blocking his path. The panther said, "You're a fool. Don't you realize the trouble you're in?"

"I know I'm in trouble when a panther is talking to me," Tree said.

"Listen to me," the panther said. "You're in danger. You know too much. You saw things tonight you weren't supposed to see. They can't let that stand. They are coming for you. Wake up your wife and run—run for your life."

"But she's sound asleep," Tree said. "I'm asleep too. It's only when I'm asleep that the panthers start to talk. If there's danger, it can wait until morning."

"No, it doesn't wait," the panther insisted. "It's here now, coming through your front door."

As though on cue, orchestrated by the panther, maestro of the unfolding nightmare, figures in brightly painted devil-masks complete with horns sprouting out of their sides, sprang into view. The panther shot away into the fire.

Strong human hands yanked Tree out of bed. A female voice cried out in the darkness. It took Tree a moment to realize the voice belonged to Freddie.

By then he was face-down on the floor, his hands yanked behind his back and bound together, beginning to understand that this was no dream.

44

The hood pulled over Tree's head closed out the nightmarish world, allowing only the sense of being hustled outside and shoved into the back of a vehicle.

Someone crowded in beside him. Doors slammed. A motor started up and then they were driving along Andy Rosse and turning right onto Captiva Drive. Logic told him they were headed off the island—what choice did kidnappers have, after all?—but his demands to know where he was being taken were met with silence.

He called out, "Freddie? Are you here? Are you all right?"

More silence except for the smooth engine sound of the vehicle. The rumble of the tires was subtly altered as they came onto the causeway. He felt the car turning left and imagined McGregor Boulevard. They seemed to drive forever along McGregor. Then, abruptly, there was another turn and then more turns and finally the car stopped.

No one moved for a time.

Finally, the back door opened and whoever was beside Tree nudged at him and grunted, "Get out." Before he could move to obey, he was being yanked outside, feeling a blast of warm Florida air as he was propelled forward. He heard a door opening and then his feet were striking hard concrete. Hands held Tree in place while other hands fumbled with the plastic strips holding his wrists together. He felt a familiar surge of relief as the blood flowed into his wrists again, and it crossed his mind that he had been tied up far too many times and he should really do something about that.

"Oh, for Christ's sake," a familiar voice said with distaste.

Tree tore off his hood, blinking into the light from a single overhead bulb. The light failed to illuminate the far corners of what appeared to be the interior of a cinderblock warehouse.

Directly below that burning light, Scratch Callister sat upright in a chair. He looked pale and ghostly, a haunted, unshaven figure in a blue track suit.

"Now I really am screwed." Scratch's voice was a resigned echo through the warehouse.

Tree stepped closer, seeing that Scratch could not easily move from the chair because his hands were tied behind him. A dozen devil-masked men spread out around the chair, keeping their distance, as though Scratch might be contaminated.

"Interesting company you keep, Scratch," Tree said.

"Aren't they just dandy? BlackHeart's finest, the Watchers contingent, particularly nasty, masked and, as usual, out for blood."

"Your blood by the look of things," Tree said.

"I'm afraid so, and I have a sad, sneaking suspicion I now understand why they have brought you here."

"Tell me," Tree said.

"Unless I miss my guess, it will be your job to defend me tonight."

"Defend you? Defend you against what?"

"Against certain ridiculous charges that have been leveled against me."

"I don't understand. Who brought charges against you?"

"The Watcher, old son. The Watcher himself. You appear to be my only hope of getting out of this, which probably means I am finished."

Lobo Salvador, without a mask, emerged from somewhere behind his masked men. "Tree, I am so glad you are here." His voice, full of warmth, was at odds with the tension in the air.

"Where is Freddie?" Tree demanded.

"I'm right here, Tree," Freddie said, coming through the door. She had been dressed in a long black robe.

"Are you all right?" he asked.

"I'm fine," she asserted. "Except for being outfitted as though I'm about to become the night's virgin sacrifice to the gods. It's a little late for that, I'm afraid."

"No one is going to harm your wife," Lobo said.

"Why have you brought us here like this?" Tree demanded.

"You wanted to find your brother, well, here he is. You can save him tonight or not. It's up to you."

"He's my half-brother," Tree said.

"Gawd, Tremain," Scratch said in exasperation. "This is no time for semantics."

"I'm not sure what I'm saving him from," Tree said to Lobo.

"Perhaps you are saving him from himself," Lobo replied. "He has betrayed those of us who once embraced him, trusted him, made us believe he is something he is not, believed he possessed powers that he doesn't possess. What's more, he defrauded our closest associates, stole their money, and generally made a mockery of us."

"That's quite a list of grievances," Tree said.

"You now understand why I want you present tonight. If there is a reason for this man to leave here alive, it's up to you to provide it."

"Whatever he's done, it's not worth the problems that are going to ensue if you kill him—kill the three of us because obviously you won't want to leave any witnesses."

"Obviously." Lobo's voice was disconcertingly agreeable.

"This is bullshit," Scratch interrupted angrily. "You can't kill me because you think I lied to you. I am exactly what I told you I am."

"No, you're not," Tree stated flatly.

"Tree, for God's sake, you're not helping." Angry bluster had been replaced by anguish.

"Tell them, Scratch," Tree advanced toward his half-brother.

"What are you talking about?"

"The secret you've held over me since we were kids, the one thing I never wanted to tell anyone."

Scratch turned his head away, as though not wanting to confront Tree.

"That night on the Sanibel beach in the midst of a rainstorm. I had just found out that the woman I thought was my aunt had been married to my father, that he had lied to me. Everyone had lied to me."

"You were very upset," Scratch confirmed. He smiled grimly. "You realized you now had a brother to deal with."

"Half-brother," Tree said. "I bolted outside into the rain, refused to go back to the cottage where we were staying. You came after me. I still wouldn't come back. You started acting crazy, dancing on the beach."

"We were both dancing, carrying on," Scratch said.

"The thunder rumbling, lightning cracking around us, and you danced and danced—like a demon, a demon in the rain. Do you remember all that?"

Scratch nodded. "Yes, of course."

"Then the lightning struck, right Scratch? It stopped everything when the lightning struck in the rain."

Scratch didn't say anything.

"But what happened? What happened that I never wanted to tell anyone? What was the secret we shared all these years, Scratch? The secret you came back to blackmail me with? What was it?"

"The lightning." Scratch's voice was barely above a whisper.

"What about the lightning, Scratch? Who was struck by the lightning?"

Scratch looked up at Tree, his eyes flashing with anger. "It was you," he breathed. "The lightning struck you, not me."

"That's right," Tree said. "It was me who got hit on the beach that night."

"We were both there when it happened," Scratch mumbled. "We both felt it."

"But I'm the one, Scratch. I should have been dead there on the beach. It knocked me to the ground, knocked the air out of me, but somehow it didn't kill me."

"It gave you something," Scratch said. "That night the lightning gave you something special that you, like the fool you've always been, refused to use."

"But that didn't stop you from taking it, using it, did it? After that night, it was you who had been struck by the lightning, and you had no trouble making that work for you."

"It might have been me," Scratch argued. "It *should* have been me. It was so close. You didn't want it. You were scared of it. Hid it so that no one would know. Like I said, a fool."

Tree swung around to Lobo. Smiling, he walked over and placed his hand on Tree's shoulder. "I should not be surprised. I sensed when we met that there was something about you, an aura. I couldn't quite put my finger on it, but it was there."

Tree pulled away from Lobo's hand. "You're as wrong about me as you were about Scratch. I was a kid who got hit by lightning on a beach. I got very lucky and survived. Now, all these years later, I'm a man, no more than that, much too human. Nothing special. Just like Scratch."

"You underestimate yourself," Lobo said quietly. "Come with us and your half-brother can go free. No hard feelings on our part."

"A deal with the devil," Tree said.

"That's one way to look at it," Lobo said.

"I don't think so, Lobo. If there is a devil here, and I don't really believe there is, it is you. Look around, you're the Watcher with the Watcher's followers. I don't think you believed that Scratch is the devil any more than I ever did. But you found him useful. You murdered Albert Aberfoyle and Kim Rada and set off the explosion that killed the Duckett brothers."

Lobo issued one of his gentle smiles. "Now why would I do that?"

"I imagine they were all in the way of you consolidating your hold on BlackHeart. The authorities will find out more about why you felt so threatened, but with Scratch around as your version of the devil, he could easily take the fall."

"'Take the fall,' I like that," Lobo said. "The old-fashioned private detective."

"Not even a very good detective," Tree said.

"Like I said, you underestimate yourself. BlackHeart is becoming a powerful, influential organization here and in Europe. You could be part of it, Tree. Join us. Become part of the darkness. It has much to recommend, believe me."

"I'm afraid I can't." Tree went over to where Scratch was seated. "My wife won't let me join anything that's dark."

"Or that forces me out of bed in the middle of the night, and makes me dress in black," Freddie added. "Not my color."

Tree lifted Scratch off the chair.

"I hate to sound melodramatic," Lobo said, "but what makes you think I am going to let you out of here?"

"You brought me here to defend my brother," Tree pointed out.

"Your half-brother," Lobo said.

"I've done that. You know what you've always suspected. Scratch is useless to you. And to my unending surprise, I have discovered late in life that I can't be bought."

"Not even for your half-brother's life?"

"Like I said before, Scratch isn't worth it. If you and your Watchers are going to take over the world, Lobo, you don't need him."

"Again, I don't want to fall back on clichés," Lobo said. "But you and Scratch know too much. I was hoping this evening would turn out differently, that you might become part of us. But since you have decided against that, well..." he allowed his voice to trail off.

Tree responded by taking Scratch's arm. "Come on, let's go home, Scratch."

"A line out of *The Searchers*, I believe," Scratch said. "Appropriate."

They started away, the devil-masked men growled to life, closing in around them.

That's when Gladys appeared, sauntering through the doorway as though it was the most natural thing in the world to be leveling a shotgun at devil-mask-wearing men in the middle of the night. "Now I can't get all you assholes," Gladys said calmly. "But the skinny prick dressed in black, he goes for certain, along with a few others as well."

"Careful, Gladys," Tree said. "Lobo here thinks he's the devil."

"That's why I brought along this Winchester Defender, one of the best pump-actions around, holds six shells loaded with double-ought buckshot, specifically designed to kill devils."

No one moved. The ensuing silence was broken by the distant sound of a siren, coming closer.

"Oh, I know what I forgot to mention," Gladys said. "Just before I got here, I called the cops."

45

"That's your big secret? You're the devil?" Rex Baxter seated at the Bimini Bait Shack's fish-tank bar was unimpressed.

"He didn't say he was the devil," Gladys corrected. She was seated on one side of Rex, Tree on the other. "He got hit by lightning as a kid, that's all."

"I prefer to think of you as the devil," Rex said to Tree. "It explains a lot of your actions over the years."

"That's exactly why I never wanted to tell anyone about what happened," Tree said. "People get the wrong impression."

"Instead, Scratch took the credit and convinced everyone that he was some sort of Satan who could change their lives," Gladys said.

"Including the Duckett brothers and their wife, Evka," Tree added.

"Who ran off to Vienna with Scratch, thus incurring the wrath of the Ducketts."

"Not to mention Lobo, who, by that time was beginning to realize Scratch was a phony who he could make use of to get rid of some of the people in BlackHeart he didn't like."

"Where is Scratch now?" Rex asked.

"As far as I know, the New Orleans police have him and are questioning him in connection with Albert Aberfoyle's Ponzi scheme," Tree said.

"And what about Evka?" Rex asked.

"The elusive Evka," Gladys said.

"She seems to have disappeared," Tree said.

"The devil is a woman," Gladys pronounced. "Or Jana Teufel is the devil. Take your pick of devils."

"I don't know about that," Rex said. "When it comes to deviltry, my money is on Tree."

A few minutes later, Gladys excused herself and went to the bathroom. Rex leaned into Tree and said, "I wanted to talk to you about Gladys."

"Okay," Tree said.

"You know we hired her as a receptionist?"

"You hired her, Rex, but yeah, I guess that was the idea."

"I mean we didn't hire her to put her in harm's way," Rex continued. "You set up that whole deal involving Lobo Salvador, right?"

"I wasn't sure what to expect, but since Lobo already had Scratch, he made it pretty clear he was coming for me."

"But you involved Gladys in the plan," Rex said.

"I couldn't have pulled it off without her keeping an eye on the house, following Lobo's people to the warehouse where they were holding Scratch, calling the police and then making her entrance in what you could only describe as the nick of time."

"That's the point. You repurpose a woman we hired to answer the phone as a gun-toting female Rambo."

"That's our Gladys, all right."

"She could have been killed."

"Gladys is a woman who knows how to take care of a lot of things, including a twelve-gauge shotgun," Tree said. "I don't think her talents are being put to the best use as a receptionist. In fact, so far they haven't been put to any use."

"Be that as it may, it's one thing for you to keep getting yourself nearly killed, and even me from time to time, but this woman is barely in the door, has hardly answered a phone call and you've got her out in the middle of the night squaring off against some sort of devil cult."

"I'm sorry, Rex, I probably should have checked with you first."

"I don't want Gladys hurt," Rex said. Softly, he added, "I really care about this woman."

"I know you do."

"You do?" Rex sounded surprised. "Has she said something to you?"

"Let's say, she knows you're interested," Tree said, choosing his words carefully.

"And?"

Tree wasn't sure what to say. Rex said, "Why are you hesitating?"

"Here's the thing, Rex. Don't you think you're a little old for her?"

Rex looked as though Tree had hit him with a baseball bat. "She thinks I'm too old?"

"She didn't say that," Tree lied.

"But that's the impression you got."

"Rex, be honest, there's a big age difference."

"Age is just a number," Rex said.

"Maybe so, but in your case, it's a pretty big number. Also, you remind me that you hired her as a receptionist, and that's fair enough. But as her employer, should you be hitting on her?"

"I'm not 'hitting on her.'" Rex sounded indignant.

"What would you call it?"

"Trying to develop a mutually satisfying relationship," Rex said.

"Fine, but you're still her employer and she's the employee and that's probably making her uncomfortable."

Rex was starting to respond when Gladys came back to the bar. She took one look at the two men and asked, "Everything all right with you guys?"

"Rex was giving me hell for getting you involved with Scratch and BlackHeart," Tree said.

"You know, Rex, I am a licensed private investigator in the state of California," Gladys said, slipping back onto her stool.

"All I'm pointing out is that we didn't hire you to get yourself killed," Rex said in a dull voice.

Gladys eyed him for a moment. "I know how to take care of myself. I'm not so sure about Tree. The idea was to make sure he didn't get himself killed."

"Which Gladys did," Tree interjected.

Rex heaved a sigh. "I'd better get back to the office. I'm supposed to meet Jerry Delson so I can listen to more of his bullshit about my book."

"That doesn't sound very good," Tree said.

"No, it doesn't," Rex said. "I'll see you later."

Tree and Gladys watched him leave. "Jerry says he's having trouble finding a publisher for Rex's book," she explained.

"It's not a goldmine after all?"

"I know Jerry can get carried away with the hyperbole," Gladys said. "But his heart's in the right place."

"I'm sure it is," Tree said.

"Jerry really is excited about Rex's book. But I think it's a generational thing. He grumbles about the kids—female kids at that—who now run publishing. They've never heard of Joan Crawford and they are only vaguely aware of someone like Hemingway."

"Joan Crawford is a small part of the book," Tree said.

"I understand that. But Jerry says it comes up a lot."

"Jerry says?"

"Yeah, we talk."

"Just talk?"

Gladys arched an eyebrow. "You're not prying into my personal life now are you Tree?"

"Not at all," Tree said. "But I do worry about Rex. I'd hate to see him hurt."

"The last thing I want is to hurt Rex. He's a sweetheart. Jerry and I have seen each other a couple of times. Drinks. Dinner. No big deal, but I like him."

"Does Rex know?"

Gladys made a face. "You know, I'd rather be coming through the door with a loaded shotgun, facing a room full of masked weirdos than dealing with those two guys."

"You're very good with the shotgun."

"Much better with a shotgun than I am with relationships," Gladys said with a sad shake of her head. "Men. My life would have been so much simpler without them."

––––––––––

After Gladys left, the Bait Shack began to fill with customers arriving for dinner. The big garage doors were open to the descending night beyond the deck. Tree sat at the bar, nursing his Diet Coke and phoning Freddie.

"I'm on my way," he said when Freddie came on the line.

"Any trouble?" she asked.

"There's not always trouble," he said defensively. "I can leave the house without getting into trouble."

"You sound a little sad, that's all."

"I'll feel better after I come home to you," Tree said.

"Then hurry."

Funny, how his mood improved simply by talking to Freddie, Tree thought as he closed down his phone and got up from the bar. A couple was waiting to take over his seat.

What was the matter with him, anyway?

Tree went down to the parking lot and got into the Mercedes. As soon as he started the engine, the back door opened and someone slipped inside and pressed the snout of a gun against his neck.

"It's like that old Raymond Chandler quote," Evka Bermann said.

"Which quote is that?" Tree asked.

"When you're not sure what's going to happen next, have a blonde enter with a gun in her hand."

Evka shoved the gun more firmly against him. "Here's the blonde with the gun," she said.

46

"We were just talking about you," Tree said, trying to keep his voice level.

"I'll bet," Evka said. "Let's go for a drive." She kept the gun pressed against him.

"Would you really shoot me right here in the Bait Shack parking lot?"

"I wouldn't take that chance if I were you."

Tree started the car forward.

"Turn onto McGregor," she ordered. "And hand me your cellphone."

"What do you want with my cellphone?"

"Just give it to me," Evka said.

As he drove onto McGregor, Tree flipped his phone back. It landed beside her on the seat. She rolled down the window and threw it out into the night.

"Hey," he said.

"Removing temptation," she announced.

"Thanks a lot," he said.

"Just keep driving," she said.

"Where are we going?"

"Let's take a ride out to Black Island."

"There's nothing there. You burned the place down, remember?"

"Just do as I tell you."

Tree glanced in the rearview mirror at Evka, her pale face caught in a series of shifting shadows.

From outside came the rumble of thunder.

By the time they reached Black Island it had begun to pelt rain.

What was left of the Duckett brothers' mansion was a dark hulk rising through the rain against a sky lit by bolts of lightning. Remnants of the police tape cautioning on-lookers not to cross fluttered in the rising wind.

Evka instructed Tree to park in the drive. The sharp odor of charred wood hung in the air. A pall of smoke like a gray mist still clung to the shell of the house.

The swimming pool that had saved his life was littered with burnt debris. Beyond the pool, a swath of inky black lawn. Thunder rumbled accompanied by more streaks of lightning that lit low-hanging black clouds like bursts of artillery fire.

Scratch Callister was all in black, a Satan beneath the umbrella he held.

"It wasn't supposed to rain," Scratch announced as Tree approached.

"I thought the New Orleans police had you," Tree said.

"Nobody 'has me,' Tremain," said Scratch as Evka left Tree to join him. "You of all people should know that by now."

"I have you," Evka said. She had put the gun away so that she could wrap herself around Scratch, the two of them together under the umbrella.

"Yes, you do," Scratch agreed. Evka held him closer.

"What are we doing out here in the rain?" Tree asked.

"Nothing very dramatic, old son. Evka and I simply wanted to say goodbye."

"Definitely say goodbye," Evka added.

"Goodbye at gunpoint," Tree said.

"I didn't want this to end without a final meeting, a closing of accounts if you will."

"There are no accounts, Scratch. Nothing to close."

"Ah, but you saved my life, old son. I'm much appreciative for that. And thanks to you, I was able to clear the decks, so to speak, get rid of the competition."

"Is that what all this was about?"

"More or less," Scratch said. "I won't say that it was all carefully planned from the outset—I wasn't really expecting to be kidnapped and held captive by Lobo Salvador I must admit, but the fact that you were able to come to my rescue, well, as I say, Tremain, it was much appreciated."

"I was merely a pawn in your long game to take over BlackHeart, is that it?"

"I think you have it, old son."

"Who killed those people? You? Or Lobo?"

"Lobo is the killer, definitely. But let's say I was able to act as a guide for him, allowing him to do the dirty work. He accomplished all that quite well, I would say."

"Then you really are the devil, Scratch."

That drew laughter. "Not me, old son. As you correctly pointed out, I am a bit of a fraud when it comes to that job. But you, Tremain, you're a different story altogether—as Lobo correctly concluded. You suffered the lightning strike; you're the anointed one. My regret is that the two of us won't be able to join forces, work together to grow BlackHeart. We would make a powerful team, let me tell you."

"That's not going to happen," Tree said. "You keep getting the wrong idea about me."

"I understand," Scratch said. "You want to be a good person and all that, although I do wonder how good you really are when it comes down to it. When the dust settles, I don't think you're any better than the rest of us."

"Maybe not, Scratch. Whatever my shortcomings, at least I keep trying."

"I'll leave it to you to continue feeding yourself the myths that apparently keep you going. It's time for Evka and me to disappear for a while. Regroup, then come back stronger than ever."

"Where do you think you're going?" Tree asked, looking around. "There is no place for the two of you to go, except maybe to a police station."

"Did I mention that I'm finished with police stations?" Scratch said.

Through the rain came the whine of an engine and a moment later the helicopter appeared out of the clouds, an iron god descending, a searchlight playing along the lawn, spinning blades lit by LED lights.

The searchlight found Scratch and Evka faces upturned, poised beneath the umbrella. The machine settled on the ground, its rotors sending the rain and the wind sideways, blowing the umbrella out of Scratch's hands. It went bouncing across the lawn.

Scratch crouched with Evka, waving at Tree. "Take care of yourself, Tremain," he shouted over the din. "We will be in touch, believe me."

The couple turned, Scratch's arm wrapped around Evka and, stooping lower, they ran together to the helicopter. A side door slid open and then they were inside, the door closing again, the helicopter almost immediately rising into the air.

The thunder grew louder and more insistent, the wind a shriek, the helicopter's searchlight bounced along the ground. Tree sank to his knees, turning his face up into the rain. The helicopter rose higher, caught in the glow of its lights, the bolt of lightning like an electric finger. The lightning stopped the helicopter, froze it against the roaring night sky for an instant before it exploded.

Burning parts of the helicopter rained down around the kneeling Tree. He lowered his head so that he did not see it crash into what was left of the Duckett mansion.

47

As Tree drove the Mercedes along the dark strip of Estero Boulevard, the rain was reduced to a drizzle. Mist had settled across the roadway, reducing visibility. He was speeding home to Freddie, hurrying away from what had just happened, dismissing any notion that he and not Mother Nature had something to do with the helicopter explosion.

He had been struck by lightning as a child and survived; that was the end of it. He had no special powers as Scratch liked to intimate. He was not the devil—played the devil a time or two in his youth in the newspaper business, possibly a few debts there to be repaid. As he kept insisting, there was nothing very special about him in the scheme of things. He had stumbled through life, messing up three marriages, losing the job he had loved more than anything, deciding on a whim to become a private investigator. What had that gotten him but a lot of grief, a couple of gunshot wounds, too many bodies and now a dead brother—*half*-brother? Power? He had no power at all. He was—

The specter bounded onto the roadway, so inky black it stood out against the dark of the night. Tree swore loudly as he swung the wheel hard. The car swerved off the road, running over the shoulder and into a rutted field. Tree fought with the wheel, stomping the brakes, finally bringing the Mercedes to a stop. He got out and ran back to the road. The black panther was caught in the glow of a light pole, poised at the side of the road, unharmed, thankfully.

The panther lowered its head, tensing its body as it prowled toward the unmoving Tree. The panther stopped a few yards away. His eyes glittered, an unblinking gaze riveted on him.

"I thought for sure you were finished," the panther said.

"Not quite," Tree replied.

"They underestimate you, Tree."

"I'm not so sure about that," Tree said.

"They don't know you," the panther said. "You fool them every time."

A single deep-throated growl and then the panther was gone, darting off and disappearing into the darkness.

Tree stood very still, allowing himself to start breathing normally again. Then he walked back to the car.

A panther talking to him, he thought, getting behind the wheel. That was too much even for him.

Or was it?

Acknowledgements

Before finally visiting Vienna, the closest I ever got to *The Third Man* was a brief introduction to Orson Welles at Ma Maison, the West Los Angeles restaurant that was all the rage and where Welles could usually be found at lunch.

By the time I met him, the comparatively slim Welles who had played the villainous Harry Lime so superbly in Carol Reed's classic adaptation of Graham Greene's story of mystery and betrayal in post-war Vienna, had long since disappeared. He had been replaced by this gargantuan, bearded figure more recognizable as the star of wine commercials than as the filmmaker who had made *Citizen Kane*, still considered to be one of the greatest, if not the greatest, movie in the history of film.

Equally, much like Orson Welles, the Vienna I associated with *The Third Man* had vanished. As Tree discovers in the book, the Vienna I encountered was a bustling, modern European city, not that much different from a lot of other modern, bustling European cities.

Also, it is difficult in Vienna to get more than a quizzical look when either Graham Greene or *The Third Man* is mentioned, although there are a couple of tours featuring sites where the movie was filmed, including, of course, the Prater amusement park where the supposedly dead Harry Lime reveals himself to Joseph Cotton's hapless Holly Martins.

And then there are the fabled sewers of Vienna where the climax of the movie was shot. They remain very much as they were when Reed filmed scenes there. It is not difficult to stand on a walkway above the tunnels and imagine Harry Lime disappearing into the gloom. However, unlike Harry, the modern visitor must wear a hard hat, a reminder that as much as you might want to be transported into *The Third Man's* shimmering black-and-white world, you are, alas, a mere tourist briefly passing through.

As first-time visitors to Vienna, I must pause here to thank Friederike Neuner for allowing my wife Kathy and me to stay in her large, welcoming Pötzleinsdorfer Strasse apartment. I can only hope she forgives me for leaving a dead body behind, a bad habit of mine when writing these books that I really must do something about.

The usual suspects once again responded to the author's desperate pleas for help: first reader and partner extraordinaire, Kathy Lenhoff; David Kendall in Belfountain, Ontario, who goes at these books with a forensic zeal; lifelong pal Ray Bennett in London; brother Ric Base in Fort Myers, Florida; sister-in-law Alexandra Lenhoff in Mississauga, Ontario; and cover designer Jennifer Smith who lives around the corner from me in Milton, Ontario. Many thanks, as well, to Quinn Sedam, Florida storm chaser and photographer, who took the extraordinary photograph used on the cover.

My single regret in preparing this book for publication is that I was not able to employ the remarkable editorial skills of Susan Holly on Sanibel Island. The Covid-19 pandemic simply did not make it feasible this time around; hopefully Susie will be back for the next novel.

Instead, a local editor, James Bryan Simpson, who did such a great job closing the latest Milton Mystery and saving the author from himself, thankfully agreed to repeat the experience—and helped make this new novel a whole lot better. Thank you, Bryan!

Lastly, I must acknowledge my debt to *The Devil and Daniel Webster*, Stephen Vincent Benét's iconic short story that first appeared in *The Saturday Evening Post* in 1936. It's been around ever since, filmed two or three times, adapted for stage and television, and even turned into a folk opera. If you are familiar with Benét's story, you will know I shamelessly stole from it. Why? What can I tell you?

The devil made me do it.

Coming Soon

THE SANIBEL SUNSET DETECTIVE SAVES THE WORLD

Only Tree Callister can do it!

Keep in touch with Ron
ronbase@ronbase.com
ronbase.com

Follow The Sanibel Sunset Detective on Facebook

Made in United States
North Haven, CT
02 September 2022

23559496R00155